JEDI SUMMER

JEDI SUMMER

by
John Boden

CEMETERY DANCE PUBLICATIONS

Baltimore
❖ 2022 ❖

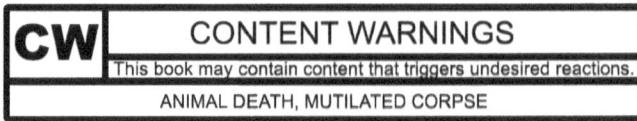

CONTENT WARNINGS
This book may contain content that triggers undesired reactions.
ANIMAL DEATH, MUTILATED CORPSE

Cemetery Dance Publications
132B Industry Lane, Unit #7
Forest Hill, MD 21050
www.cemeterydance.com

This is for my baby brother Ross,
I love you and am so proud of the man you've become.

FOREWARD

WHAT IS it about coming-of-age tales that readers of dark fiction find so appealing? Why does it seem like every horror writer wants to try his or her hand at penning at least *one?*

I think it's a longing for better days. Things are tough all over, and things are scary everywhere…but remember how much tougher and scarier life was when we were children? Or so we thought. Back then, we were so sure it could only get better once we were all grown-up. Adults had the freedom to do the things they wanted to do. They just seemed to have it all together, didn't they? Little did we know what awaits us when we get older: responsibilities, bills to pay, mouths to feed besides our own, health issues as we journey closer to the grave with every passing second.

I think that's why we enjoy a good coming-of-age tale. Because we've been there, when the world seemed so much larger and infinitely more terrifying. We were warned again and again that we should never talk to strangers (although we were never told, thank God, exactly what a stranger would do to you if you dared to give him the time of day)…we knew hungry things lurked in the dark that weren't there in the daylight (it's why we never slept with one foot hanging out of the covers, no way!), and we couldn't wait to become adults so we would be privy to whatever secret they all knew that kept them so aloof and unafraid and...adult.

Who am I kidding. We couldn't wait to grow up simply because we yearned to do all of the things adults got to do because they were adults.

We didn't know how good we had it, back then.

We had no idea that there are worse things than waiting.

Remember how it always felt like a large chunk of your childhood was spent *waiting?* Waiting for that half hour to pass after lunch so you could jump back in the pool (because every parent insisted you would drown if you didn't wait, just like they promised if you made an ugly face it would stay like that forever—see what I mean about how *terrifying* it was to be a kid?)...waiting for a "yes" from Mom or Dad when you asked if your best friend could sleep over (it was never as much fun as you imagined it would be when you first came up with the idea, and despite your plans to stay awake all night you were both asleep before nine)...waiting for the man on the radio to announce that, yes, your school was one of several that was closed for the day due to snow (wasn't *that* the greatest thing ever, before adulthood came along and taught us you still have to drive in that mess?)...waiting to be old enough to do the things your older sibling never missed out on ("but, Mom, it's so unfair! Just 'cause she's sixteen she gets to do whatever she wants!")...and of course, waiting for your favorite movie to hit the local theater.

As dark and disturbing as the subject matter of John Boden's *Jedi Summer* can be at times, it is the characters' excitement for ~~the latest installment in the greatest movie series of all time~~...er, sorry, hyperbole slipping in there...*Return of the Jedi* that looms over this story like a roiling storm cloud. If you're like me and you don't mind a good summer storm. If you consider the sight of a storm cloud to be a pretty cool thing.

Jedi Summer is a snapshot of one special moment in time. It is an unconventional coming-of-age tale like nothing I have ever read before. In some ways, it is a collected series of vignettes that have nothing and at the same time *everything* to do with one another. It is a fictional memoir inspired by every classic coming-of-age tale that has come before it (although some of it *did* really happen, according to the author—if one day he chooses to share which parts are fiction and which aren't, that is entirely up to him). And yet, *Jedi Summer* is its own strange beast. At times a weird, wistful, stream-of-consciousness novella that could only have been written by the author of *Dominoes*, it is nothing if not extremely engaging from the first sentence to the last.

Just like when I was a kid, I found myself waiting...waiting to see what came next with an urgency that was almost agonizing.

And at the same time, I dreaded to see it all come to an end.

Savor this one, like we all should have savored the best years of our lives. You'll be glad you did.

James Newman
April 8, 2016

PART I

NOW

IT SEEMS *to me, that with these sorts of books, these coming-of-age works, the protagonist usually grows up to become a mega-successful author or something and then, in a reflective coup against his publisher, stows away in a cabin somewhere and pens his memoirs. Plied with copious amounts of bourbon and enough self-loathing and guilt to choke a tiger. Only to turn the manuscript into something that will not only win over the staunchest of critics, but most likely win Rob Reiner a fucking Oscar...again. Like Meathead needs another statue.*

This isn't that shit. Not at all.

I'm not a successful author. I have a handful of short stories I've sold and a day job baking pies and cakes at a grocery store. I count my pieces of silver at the cost of your waistline and blood sugar levels. I just feel that I have some neat things to share, cool and uncool alike. We all have a voice. No one is more important than any other. We all have stories and histories, writ in dirt and sweat and tears and dust. Miles of Bibles beneath our skin.

We all like to make a collage of memory, situating the best and worst of them into logistical clusters. We also wish we could take the really bad ones and crumple them, toss them aside like the sharp refuse they feel like.

But you can't do that...

Could you remain standing if you threw away your ankle or your knee cap? Sure, you could adapt and learn, but it would take a while. I'm not at all certain of where I was going with that metaphor so let me swing with this...we are all living collages, sculptures in progress. We are made up of what we've been through and what lies ahead. How we react, reacted and will someday react. We carve each wrinkle and every bulge or bone. Some self-made Prometheus. Beautifully hideous and horrifically gorgeous. Gods, actually. Sage and stony. Often stupid.

We are history, and we are memories. Here are some of mine:

THE NEXT TO THE LAST WEEK OF SCHOOL

- 1 -

AFTER YEARS and years of not having one, this year, we finally had a home of our own. I mean all ours. No rent checks to deliver or landlords to hassle with. Until this pivotal moment, all we had ever known and lived in were rented trailers...

[We were renting a mobile home about a mile out of town, further out than our Gram lived. It was a sad affair; a run-down trailer the landlord had tried to spruce up by adding on a larger room from the side. This, he accomplished by literally cutting an enormous hole in the side of the trailer and then adjoining a large

wooden box. It worked. I mean, it was drafty when the weather turned but it gave us a large living room, one that I sprawled on the floor of for many hours, soaking up TV airings of The Exorcist *and* Tentacles. *This was the year of Three Mile Island. An incident that made my mother cry, I paid it no mind. I was nine-years-old, so as long as it didn't fuck up the air time of* The Dukes of Hazzard *or anything, I was good.*

That winter, Roscoe and I wanted Star Wars *figures...everyone did. And we woke Christmas morning to find we had gotten some. In our excitement and ecstasy over this event, we began to stomp and jump and carry on. That ceased as soon as we heard a loud crack and groan and when the living room dropped about three feet from the rest of the room.*

To this day, I use this event as a benchmark of poor upbringing. Someone will say "We grew up so poor....blah blah blah" and I usually listen, smirk and say "Did your living room ever fall off of the trailer on Christmas day?" This usually gets nothing but an uncomfortable look wherein I jab the boot in with "I win." and go about my business...]

...and ramshackle houses. But this one was ours, well, Mom's. It sat on the hill at the end of town, and it was ours. I still had to share a room with my little brother, but I was used to it. It was all I had ever known. But the room was larger than a closet, which was a decided step up from what we'd always had. Our bunk bed was the central focal point of the room and the walls were lined with a few bookshelves, a dilapidated dresser and a small desk. An old coffee table nestled behind the door held my hand-me-down stereo system. The walls were plastered with posters from music magazines and horror movies. I did allow my little brother a few identity markers in the room: his poster for *The Last Unicorn*, his numerous stuffed animals, and the damned Legos that I stepped on in my bare feet every night. We had a home and a real bedroom. It was ours. We were happy.

- 2 -

THE STREETLIGHT outside our window made it difficult to sleep. There was always the dull hum of it wafting through the screen on the breeze. The room was never truly dark. Having a little brother in the bunk beneath you didn't help much either. I'm lucky I've never required much shut-eye. Of course, maybe this is where I developed the ability to function on little sleep.

"Johnny," his little voice whispered from below.

I ignored him, pulling the afghan over my head to dowse the light. The tiny fibers from the acrylic yarn tickled my nose. It smelled, mildly, of sweat and cat. Epiphany always chose my bed for her slumber. I named her after the character in William Hjortberg's novel, *Falling Angel.* She was a small calico but lighter than most tortoise shell cats—a pale gray and orange so light it looked pink. She was a beautiful cat.

"Johnny, you wanna know what?" Roscoe insisted.

I sighed heavily, something I had always done and never knew it would become my trademark in adulthood. I also never realized every sigh was a needle prick to my little brother. It was a tiny pinch on the back of the arm that meant *"You are annoying and bothersome."* I did it often and without any thought. His arms covered with unseeable bruises and welts that would never really disappear.

"What?" I snarled. Headlights blazed through the window and off the glossy surface of my DURAN DURAN poster as a car cruised by. "What?" I said a little louder, tailed with another sigh. 'Piph was sleeping between my feet and leapt at the noise, running from the room. She'd return soon enough, she always did.

"Um. You know that quiet isn't really quiet." My little brother paused, awaiting some signal to continue which I failed to provide, so with trepidation, he continued. "It never is. Even when it's quiet. The quiet is sorta noisy. Sounds like little mouths eating little crackers." I edged the afghan from my face and thought on this. It was true. Just like if you peered hard enough into empty space, you could convince yourself you could see the air. Subconscious illusion born of the frustration from trying to put a mask on the invisible. I smiled. The little boy beneath me had no idea how brilliant he was, I don't think he ever would. He just wanted to impress his big brother.

"You're right, Roscoe. That's pretty smart," I encouraged. I was startled when my other cat, Bandit jumped on the bed and took her daughter's spot between my feet. "Now, get to sleep, we have school tomorrow. This is the last week before summer vacation." I rolled over and listened to Roscoe whispering goodnight to his pets. I closed stinging, tired eyes and went to sleep. Roscoe hummed to himself as I began to drift. The dreams I had I could not remember. Maybe, I had none at all.

- 3 -

MOM WAS at work when I woke up. Nothing unusual there. Often times, she'd get home from one job after Roscoe and I were in bed, and would be up and off to the other before we rose in the morning.

[She worked three jobs. Night nurse at a nearby hospital, tending bar at the American Legion on weekends, and she cleaned houses in whatever slivers of time remained. She had managed to shoehorn shifts at the local sewing factory in there for a while before it shut down.]

I fixed Roscoe some breakfast—a bowl of cereal. The last time I had tried to make him eggs, and he told Mom I had fed him runny, gross eggs. He claimed they weren't done and I wouldn't let him get up from the table until he ate them. This was all true, of course. I was almost thirteen, and he was lucky I had made the attempt. "Here, Kris," Roscoe called as he dropped a piece of his toast on the floor under the table. I stared at him and frowned a bit. Kris was our Gram's dog and he'd been dead at least two years. Roscoe had been feeding him ever since.

"When does *Jedi* come to the movies?" Roscoe asked as I poured the cereal into his orange plastic bowl. He was smiling big, with his eyes.

"You remember when Mom took us to see *Empire Strikes Back*?" He spoke over a too-large mouthful of milky cereal. A small spray of milk peppered the tablecloth.

"I sure do." I smiled then, remembering.

[We had lived at the other house then. One of the many other houses. A large white affair faded to cataract gray on the corner of Gunnells Street. We rented it. Until now, we had always rented. It was Roscoe, Mom and I, and her alcoholic boyfriend, Bob. He was nice. He looked a little like James Brolin in The Amityville Horror. *He played with us and couldn't hold a job, which was more than likely why he was always around to play with us. He drank a lot of the time and played guitar. He was usually a happy drunk, until the happy drunk got drunk. Then, he got angry. Then, hands turned to fists. Never for us, though. I think for Mom a few times.*

One night, he walked up the street to the Legion and got his drink on. He was bringing home pizza for us when he stumbled and dropped it in the street. Mom went out to see what the ruckus was about and the next thing I knew, there were flashing lights and the lady who lived across the street was taking Roscoe and I over to her house. I sat on her couch and watched the end of Moonraker. *Roscoe slept in her recliner. Gram came and got us and we went to her house. I'm not sure I was ever clued in to what really went down, All I know is Bob was never around after that.*

Anyway, we were pretty happy. Mom worried as she did but we got by. She took us to see Empire *when it came to our area. We were so excited and the movie was mind-blowing. Roscoe and I*

played it out in the backyard for months until we moved—again—
to a dumpy red house down in the darkest corner of town.]

"It comes out next Friday. But it probably won't come around here for another month or so. That's the price we pay for living in the boonies."

I poured the milk on my own breakfast. Thank God, it was real milk this week. We had been forced on occasion to use powdered milk, and—unlike the Government cheese, which was delicious—that shit isn't fit for human consumption. We sat at the table and ate our Golden Grahams and watched the clock above the refrigerator. Its electric whine was lost amidst the crunch of cereal and the smacking of dairy-wet lips.

"I hate the boonies," Roscoe piped up as he shoveled another spoonful into his mouth. Milk dribbled down his chin. "When do we hafta leave?" he asked through soggy cereal.

"About ten minutes," I responded. I bent to pick up the toast Roscoe had thrown on the floor for the dead dog. There was a corner missing and no butter left on it. It was soggy. I grimaced as I dropped it in the trash can.

"I don't want to go, I think I'm sick." I rolled my eyes as Roscoe put on a tired face. He pulled this shit three times a week. "I think I'm burning up."

"Shut up, whiner. You're fine. It's the last week of school. Don't be an asshole." I sat my bowl in the sink after I rinsed it.

"I'm telling, you swearer!" The tired face morphed once again, this time into a jubilant grin.

That kid loved to tattle more than anything. I sneered at him and raised my hand like I was going to slap him but didn't. He flinched.

"Good. When don't you? Let's go." I took his bowl as he went to get his shoes on.

'Go brush your teeth!" I yelled and stood in place until I heard him stomping up the stairs. I went into the living room and took off the shirt Mom had laid out for me. It was a striped shirt which was quite in fashion, but not when said stripes were pastel in color—lavender and sunshine yellow. Mom had made it for me from scraps she'd gotten from the sewing factory. I never told her I didn't like it. She was so pleased with her work and I was appreciative, just not enough to wear a pastel striped shirt to high school. I stashed the shirt under the couch cushion and pulled on a ratty ZZ TOP shirt. "Now," I screamed. I grabbed my Walkman and the radio mix tape from the stereo cabinet and waited.

[*You will never understand the triumphant joy and work that went into making a mix tape in the early '80s. You had to literally sit by the radio, for hours, and wait for them to play the song you wanted. PAUSE, PLAY, and RECORD buttons all pushed down and waiting. The DJ would yap, usually well into the beginning of the song you were waiting for, and then as soon as he shut the fuck up, you clicked off the PAUSE button and you were recording. When all was said and done, you had sixty shitty minutes of chopped and diced pop glory. You had "The Safety Dance" with about 4 seconds of the DJ blathering about the weather as an intro. Or you had a version of "Take Me To Heart" that slid into the first few notes of "Islands In The Stream" which cut suddenly because you didn't like that song. Hell, yeah, the '80s!*]*

I grabbed the frayed black gym bag I used to carry books and slid my school stuff inside.

"C'mon!" I yowled, and started for the back door. I was at the bottom of the hill by the time Roscoe came storming out. "Did you turn the lock?" I asked. He nodded and hustled to catch up. "Are you sure?"

He nodded again. A thin ring of toothpaste surrounding his lips. "Wait here and wipe your face." I sighed, and stomped back up the steps and checked the door. Locked. As he took his place beside me, I smacked him upside the head.

"Jeez!" He winced and rubbed his head as though I had cracked him with a wrench instead of my open hand. "I said it was locked," he whined.

We walked to the bus stop. I tried to keep a reasonable distance between my little brother and me. I had appearances to maintain.

The air smelled smoky. Zinoble's must have been burning brush over the hill, a smell I would forever associate with Halloween, for some reason.

- 4 -

I SOMETIMES referred to Roscoe as "The Magnetic Kid."

Not because he walked around with soda cans and bolts sticking to his skin, although that would have been amusing. The reason behind his nickname was a bit stranger and based on an anecdote from our gram.

Our grandmother was the town Avon lady. She did okay with it, but I always felt she did it more for the opportunity to drive around and gossip; a chance to talk with the ladies of the town rather than her deep-seated concern for lack of cosmetic enhancement. She was a great and kind woman, known to take no money if she knew her customer was struggling. All heart, that was our gram.

One day, Gram was sitting on the porch talking to Penny Holden. Penny had just come back from a stay in the hospital following a mild stroke. She told my gram about seeing Roscoe walking to the store earlier. "That boy and them animals," Penny chuckled, a sweet throaty rattle hanging on her laughter. She smoothed a fold in her dress and waved as a car tooted its horn in passing. Small town salutations.

"What animals?" Gram asked, taking a deep drag on her ever-present cigarette. Marlboro Light 100s, I still remember.

"Them dogs and cats. Always trailin' that boy. Like a tail on a kite." Penny paused and looked off into the lilacs flanking the porch. "Three dogs, I think, and some cats. All gray, like faded pictures. That one dog is a homely one. His ass end higher than his front.

Unfortunate mutt he is. So ugly he's cute." She smiled wide, showing dentures that needed a proper cleaning and seemed too large for her drawn face. Her laughter fluttered on the breeze like confetti.

Inside my gram's mind, wheels were turning. The dog Penny had described was dear ol' Tippy, a mutt so strangely put together, it had to be a joke. He had dachshund and terrier in that mix somewhere. He was the friendliest, most loving and affectionate dog we had ever owned. He had also been shot by a neighbor and died the previous autumn.

[Tippy had come into town from out at Gram's, a trek he made often. It was nearly a two-mile journey and the little dog would bound through pasture and wood to arrive at our house. Never was sure how he knew where we lived. He would stand on our back step and yip and whine until we came out to play or corralled him until Gram could drive in and get him. This time, we weren't home and he got bored and meandered down the block. A man that lived there shot him. Poor Tippy then dragged himself to our house, leaving bloodstains on the concrete steps, and when we didn't answer his whining, he dragged himself the distance back out to Gram's. I was home by the time she called me and told me what had apparently transpired. Had I gone in the back door, I might have seen the blood and figured something was wrong. I didn't. He'd been shot in the side and had worn all the meat from his belly dragging himself home. We had to take him to be put down and that drive to the vet's with the dying dog laying quietly on my lap; that did me in for dog owning from that point on. His little dry nose on my hand, rooting so the contact wouldn't be broken, tiny bursts of hot breath against my palm until it…he stopped. In a lot of ways, I did too.]

Gram smiled but it was a bit uneasy this time. She lit another cigarette and dropped her lighter into the purse at her feet.

"Oh," was all she could manage. The smoke calmed her little. An annoying phantom feather at her face.

"They love that boy. They just follow him like a shadow. Like he was a magnet." Penny shifted on her chair and stood shakily. "You wanna come in for some tea, Barb?"

"No, thanks. I have to go finish delivering this Avon," she replied as she descended the wooden steps. "I'll see you, Penny. Hope you're feelin' better." Penny waved as she opened the screen door and Gram took a step towards her green Chevy at the curb.

"Tell that other grandson of yours to come by and bring me some of his stories. I read that poem he had in the arts festival the other summer. He's talented," Penny called as Gram slid into her dirty car.

"Okay," Gram called back and pulled away from the curb and down the street. Penny waved once more before disappearing into her home.

Gram told me all of this later that evening, while we waited for Roscoe to come out of the house. It would be almost another week before she would relay the message to me, about Penny wanting me to stop by with some of my writing. And I would shyly come up with a few dozen excuses to never do so. I was always weird about grown-ups reading my stuff.

Penny never sat on her porch and gazed at her lilacs again. In fact, she never made it through that summer. A bigger stroke carried her off on the Fourth of July, as she sat on her porch listening to all the rifle shots and bottle rockets bursting in mid-air.

Twenty-five years later, Gram would go the same way. On Memorial Day.

- 5 -

THOSE LAST nine school days flew by, unless you were sitting at your desk watching the clock. Then, they crawled like a slug on its way to the salt mines. Yet, before we knew it, it was Wednesday morning. The last day of school. We had to make it to lunchtime and then we were free. For a few months. If we'd known then what adulthood was truly like, we'd have savored every minute of every sun-drenched day for the sumptuous morsel it was. Being children, we scarfed them down, greedily, like so many potato chips or snack cakes. Never to be full.

The important thing was that school had ended, though sadly not in the Alice Cooper predicted explosive fashion we always hoped for, so we turned in our worn books, scrubbed the pencil and ink from our desks, and said goodbye to our teachers. Threw away all the carcasses of notebooks and tablets that had valiantly given their innards for the noble pursuit of knowledge (or more accurately, wasted minutes of doodling or note-writing. The notebook covers now faded skin tattooed with sentiments like *VAN HALEN RULEZ!* or *DF + TN 4EVER*). We tossed them into the large bin until our desks and lockers were empty. It took days for those last fifteen minutes to ooze by. Then the bell rang. The clanging of salvation.

The bus ride home was excruciating. Everyone was so anxious to completely shake the bonds of the educational prison. We were inmates who had finally escaped. I looked at my gym bag, bulging with the contents of my locker—a school year's amount of old papers and worksheets, workbooks, and ratty folders; I never could bear to throw it all away like the others. The special joy I would reap from feeding that shit to the barrel the next time I burned trash was unparalleled. I had also neglected to turn in the copy of *The Golden Apple of the Sun*, a Ray Bradbury book I had borrowed from my English teacher, Mrs. Robinson. I read it at least six times that school year and could not bear to give it back.

[*I still have this Bradbury paperback. It is one of my most cherished books.*]

The bus slowed, and the brakes screeched. The driver, Dew, hollered at a few of us by name, letting us know it was our stop. He had driven many of our parents and often used this to his disciplinary advantage. I got off and sat on the Roses' porch, watching as Roscoe made his way up the street, the elementary school being only across the bridge while mine was miles away. I had started middle school that year. I don't want to talk much about that.

So, I sat on that front step and waited for Roscoe to catch up. He walked slowly, muttering to himself the entire time. His untied shoelaces danced about his feet like writhing worms.

"Hi," he said, breathing a bit heavy as he struggled to keep up. We mounted the hill where our house squatted on top, like a giant brick toad.

"How was the last day?" I asked.

"Great." He smiled widely. "We gave the teacher our books, and she put them in boxes. Then we got to play outside until it was lunch." He paused and gulped some summery air. "We had cup-cakes. Tony's mom made 'em." I would have been able to figure this out sans admission by the ring of dried icing that lined his lips and the few blobs of icing on the neck of his faded He-Man shirt. He was a heavy-set kid and winded easily, but he never let that hinder his trying to keep up.

"Only we didn't have lunch, it was the end of the day at lunch-time today. So we got to leave." He looked behind him and down at the ground. "Keep up, Kris," he scolded.

I looked back and almost imagined I could see the ghost of Gram's long departed cocker spaniel.

"Maybe I can have some Oodles of Noodles when we get home?" he asked, squinting at me in the sun. "It's summer now." Roscoe beamed. All I did was nod.

I hoped he could always be as happy as he was at that moment. Sometimes hope can be enough.

[It was this picture of my younger sibling that I would file away in the ol' memory bank. It would be this smiling face I would see whenever I thought of him going through all the struggles and jumping the hurdles and stones that life was going to throw at him. And, sadly, he would be thrown a lot. When I talk to him on the phone or chat on Facebook with him, I always see that boy. Round cheeks and that cowlicky hair. I love him, and I never tell him enough. I don't suspect I ever will.]

"It sure is. Let's get home and change, then we can slide down the dirt hill." This was one of our more notorious pastimes. It consisted of trudging up the very steep bank behind the closed auto garage. Once at the top, we would sit in a cardboard box and slide down the loose dirt and stones and try to make it to the bottom unscathed. Sledding, redneck kid style. It was a ridiculously silly and dangerous game, but we were kids in a tiny town with nothing else to do.

"Yeah, to the dirt hill!" Roscoe yelled, and with that we broke into a run.

Above us, the sun smiled, too. Giggles floated through the air like strange birds.

- 6 -

THAT FIRST week of summer vacation was always the best. We were up with the sun and outside playing until after dusk. We ran the woods like something out of *Lord of the Flies*. We climbed trees and tackled that damn dirt hill. And we fought. My little brother and I were always at each other. I will admit, now, that I did my best to antagonize the hot-tempered little shit.

I might have nailed his Skeletor action figure to the tree in the backyard. I may have rubbed his favorite stuffed animal on my crotch and told him it was gay. It is possible I may have once told him the words "slight scoliosis" (written on his school physical health report) meant he was in fact stricken with an alien disease and would die. I did all of these things, but I also did my best to help raise him while Mom worked her numerous jobs, with little complaint.

I may have called him slow and stupid and a million other unkind names. But I didn't really mean it. Not in any long-term hateful kind of way. Kids are kids, and by that I say kids are stupid. Kids are assholes. We don't get that those things have an echo. Words are boomerangs. It would be almost thirty years before my brother would let me know that those things caused wounds, and that revelation would make me feel horrible. I still do.

But at the time, I was being a snotty near-teenager, which would give way to being a sarcastic young man. He was an annoying seven-year-old. We loved to hate each other and hated to love one another, yet we did both without quite knowing it. Most of the time, we were all we had.

"Look at those birds," Roscoe crowed one evening as we sat on the back step, eating Otter Pops. The moths and bugs were a crowding cloud around the lighted area where we sat.

"Those are bats" I said, as we watched the dive-bombing shadows pick the insects from the air.

"Like Dracula?" he asked, smiling proudly with a green sticky grin. "Or the blue guy from *Salem's Lot*?" His smile grew wider, making his brown eyes squint.

"Not quite," I answered. He knew my love for all things scary and tried to work in what he knew when he could. I loved it. It made me proud. "C'mon. Let's go get your bath so we can watch a video before going to bed."

"Can we watch *Beastmaster* or maybe *The Last Unicorn*? I always watch the scary ones you like; lemme watch one." His eyes were shining with excitement. And I did love that stupid movie almost as much as he did. The Vore were scarier than most creatures in straight horror films.

"Okay. *Beastmaster*."

"Do we have barbeque chips and soda?"

"Yeah, Mom got a barrel when she got groceries and Gram brought us some soda earlier," I said.

"Woo-hoo!" he bellowed and jumped up from the cement. HHJe was inside and the door was slamming before I had even gotten to my feet.

The moon was up and looked nearly red. I heard the cows groaning over the hill and across the street I could see the glow of Mr. Cowell's cigarette as he stood on his porch. I went inside and closed the door. As per Mom's explicit instructions about the nights she worked, I locked it with the chain as well. I watched through sheer curtains until Mr. Cowell's cigarette winked out like an eye, and then I went upstairs and drew Roscoe's bath.

- 7 -

MOM WORKED overnight at the hospital and on days when she was sleeping, we'd head out for Gram's after we got up. It was a two-mile hike over the hill and through the pastures and woods, but we had done it a million times. We'd play out there all day and Gram would drive us back in to town later on. I liked watching her soap operas— her "stories"—with her while having tea and cinnamon toast.

["Johnny, will you shush? As the World Turns *is coming on."] I'd hear that at least a hundred times that summer.]*

Sometimes, we'd have chocolate pudding in the little metal cans or foil shrouded TV dinners. She had too many cats and smoked too much, but that woman was the greatest. She had a kind heart and a sweet soul. She would do anything for anybody. I'm not sure it was as appreciated as much as it should have been.

This morning started like all of those others, but it didn't stay that way.

We had crossed the road and ran over the hill to the pastures. We ran by cows and dodged their plops with an efficiency born of practice. We scuttled through a little wooded area that crested into another small hill, and on the other side of that hill sat Gram's trailer.

Roscoe was in the lead and had just entered the gulley when he stopped dead. I heard a cow moo. It didn't sound right. Very dry and ragged. And there was a smell. It smelled meaty and thick and a little like rotten garbage. In the pocket of silence, I heard buzzing. I stopped as well and grabbed Roscoe's arm when I saw it. He was shaking. Terrified. His skin was cold in spite of the heat of the day.

"What's wrong with it?" Roscoe could not contain his revulsion. His face was drawn and pale. His little hands were balled into fists at his sides. He dug his sneakers into the dirt and looked at me, begging me to do something.

"Johnny! What happened to it?" His voice was wet with tears. But all I could do was stare as well.

My mouth was in drought. This pitiful thing stood there staring at us. "It's sick," I said, having no idea how to explain to this boy what the real problem was. My stomach lurched and my breakfast bowl of Cookie Crisp threatened to vacate the premises. The smell was almost visibly thick and the buzzing was deafening.

The problem was that a mother cow had trundled off to deliver her calf, but the calf was breach and had gotten stuck and died mid-birth. This tragic animal was now standing before us with a dead calf hanging halfway out of her. Flies fought for their claim. The cow was in a bad way. Her rheumy wet eyes that seemed to plead for help. Its snout was drenched with mucus and tears. Her heart broken and her body dying. I felt my own eyes tearing up.

"Let's go tell Gram," I said, and we fled.

The cow let loose another sad wail. I swear it said, "Help me." My stomach was screaming by the time we got to Gram's porch. And I couldn't see through the tears in my eyes.

Gram called Orlando, her landlord and owner of the cattle. She told him what we'd seen, and he informed her he'd been missing that cow for a few days. She had gotten out of the fenced in section where the rest of the herd was and must've gone off to deliver. He'd be right there to take care of it. "He's coming," was all Gram said as she hung the receiver back on its fork.

Roscoe and I were on the swing eating freeze pops when Orlando's truck pulled into the driveway. He got out and grabbed a rifle from the back. He walked right past us and the trailer and up over the bank. He was a large but friendly man; the look on his face that morning would never convey that. He avoided any eye contact and did not speak. He ate up the distance with his giant strides.

For about thirty seconds all sound was sucked out of the valley. Nothing. No birds or breeze or cows or grasshoppers, but absolute quiet.

Until...

The shot sounded like thunder in an oil drum. "What did he do?" Roscoe asked, still shaking a little, his eyes wide. His lips were blue from his icy snack. "Johnny?"

"He helped it," was all I could say, my voice cracking.

Gram stood at the screen door, her own eyes wet with tears. No amount of popsicles, swinging, or cartoons could salvage that day.

- 8 -

WITHOUT SCHOOL, the days were an endless tapestry of playing outside and watching scary movies. I had stopped attending church, not because I shunned any faith or anything like that, but because some of the people thought it was more important how you dressed for services than the fact you were there at all. We were poor and could not afford dressy attire. I would go to Sunday school or church in nice jeans and a sweater or button-down shirt, which seemed fine to me. But apparently there is a religious acceptance dress code somewhere that I was not following. After overhearing a few snide comments one Sunday, I quit going. Faith is a personal thing, between you and your deity. Anywhere, anytime, and wearing anything. It truly is that simple.

Sunday was a high point for another reason. It was farm day. We got to drive an hour and spend the afternoon at my great-grandparents' farm. Playing in the barns and sheds or running in the fields. We'd visit my cousin who lived nearby. I always enjoyed those times. I always liked to sit and listen to the adults talk. Loved hearing stories from my grandparents. Learning special facts. I found out the area where the dam stood currently and what would grow to become Lake Raystown Resort was once owned by my pap and another farmer. That the government had come and offered them a small sum in the early '70s. They turned it down, only to have the government return a few years later and take the land they wanted and pay them a lesser amount under some kind of "domain" law or something. The government was shady, I learned. Shit, I'm still learning that. I found that the lake is now covering what was once miles of farm land, that it holds entire farms within its depths. Intact houses and barns, old cars, and tractors all untouched beneath countless gallons of water.

[*When I was a kid, there was a tale that circulated about a man who drowned in the lake. He had gone missing, and they found his fishing boat and gear, so he was presumed to have fallen overboard. After a few days with no body surfacing, the Police Department sent divers down into the chilly depths to look for a cadaver. According to lore, after a few hours the divers surfaced and vowed never to go back down again, claiming they saw catfish and muskellunge down there bigger than they were. One stated a fish was swimming near an old Chevy that was on the bottom and was nearly twice as long as the damned car! They never recovered the man's corpse. True or not, I never even so much as waded in that lake again.*]

When I wasn't eavesdropping or playing outside at the farm, I'd sit in my pap's recliner and read his Zane Grey books or Gramma's *Ellery Queen* magazines. I think some of my formative reading began in that chair, reading *Alfred Hitchcock Presents* while trying not to smell or look at my grandfather's spit can.

PART II

THE LAST WEEK OF JUNE

- 1 -

WE HAD just come home from a weekend at our dad's. It was usually nice to see him and my stepmom and stepsisters. We always ended up spending more time with them than anyone, since my dad and stepmom both worked. But we shared meals and then Dad would usually stake his plot on the couch and put on baseball or football, although watching is sort of interpretive, since he'd usually nod off within the hour, leaving us to either play outside or, in my case, sit in the kitchen and read or write stories.

If I'm to be honest, at the time, I resented this. I hated that I had to go there every other weekend to do the same shit I could do at home. I grew resentful of my dad for just sitting around and watching sports that I had no interest in. If I knew then how fickle life was and that one day I'd be sitting in that very room, holding my father's hand as he died, things would have been decidedly different. I would have happily sat through every goddamn baseball game, every weekend for a hundred summers.

But at the time, I had no idea what working swing shifts does to a person. I had no clue how tired and irritable you become. These were things I would learn first-hand in adulthood. And the crow I would eat would leave a bitterness in my mouth that would never fully wash away.

"We're home," Roscoe yelled as we bounced in the back door.

Mom stood in the kitchen with a cigarette in her hand and a cup of coffee in the other. The worried grimace on her face changed to a big smile, not quite fast enough to cement sincerity. "Hi, guys. Did you have a nice time at your dad's?" Drag...gulp.

"It was okay. Same old boredom. I wrote a new story," I offered.

"Cool. What's it about?"

Besides my English teacher, my mother was one of the only grown-ups who seemed interested in the fact that I enjoyed writing. She is still my number one fan.

"A vampire vacuum-cleaner," I revealed.

[I actually wrote this story. It was entitled "Hoover From Hell" and was maybe a single page, typed. I was quite confident I had written the niftiest story ever penned by a twelve-year-old. I was so taken by my amazing talents that I went to the library and Xeroxed a copy of it and sent it to Stephen King.

Swear to God, I was that lame.

But the best part came almost a year later, when I went for the mail and discovered a small envelope addressed to me. Inside

*was a small yellow postcard, pre-printed with a little "thank you
for writing" spiel and credited to Stephen King. It was quite cool.
What kicked cool off the chair and left it gasping in a noose was
what was on the back. Hand written in red ink was a small note:
"This is fun. I certainly look forward to reading more of your
work someday. Thanks, S.K."*

*I ran home like my heels had wings. I showed that card to
everyone for months. And it hung on the corkboard over my desk
until I left for college, years later. Unfortunately, when my mother
re-married and sold the house, the card was lost in the transition.
But the joy of hearing from an influence or idol is simply unparalleled. I have since had the pleasure of meeting many, counting
them as friends, and it is still quite amazing.]*

"Really?" She laughed, paused and smiled. "That's great. Can
I read it?"

"Not yet," I said. I headed for my room with my notebook and
my borrowed copy of *The Dead Zone.*

"And how about you, Roscoe? How was your weekend?"

"Fine. We had spaghetti, and we played outside with the cars
and played kickball. I fell asleep in the car on the way to the store,
and Johnny and the girls made fun of me."

"Don't worry about it. Go put your stuff away."

"Okay." And with a few stomping steps he was gone.

Mom's face reverted to its true state. A slightly pained and
sad expression she would never fully shake. Always full of worry
and regret, never absorbing the fact she was a great mother who
did what was needed to provide for us. Working three jobs.
Whatever. To her it was all shortcoming and failure. It was swimming up for a desperate breath from deep, icy water and getting
within lip's reach of the surface only to begin to sink again. It
was never enough.

A lot of the time, she made my heart hurt.

- 2 -

THE WEATHER was nice and the night warm. I often liked to stay up late and write. I would plug in my enormous electric typewriter and drag it out on to the porch roof, through my bedroom window. I would then angle the desk lamp to shine out and lay on the cool shingles and type away. I wrote numerous stories on that roof. Even now, when I drive through town, I look at our old house and hope the folks who live there realize all the special things that happened there. Houses are as much a part of us as family. They watch us grow, keep us safe, and protect us. And then one day, we leave them. A tragic loop we play over and over, in differing facets of our lives.

I was lying on my stomach, a pillow under my torso, typing away. I missed my old manual typewriter, but this one was considerably lighter to deal with. This story was about a flood. A boy and his mother, trapped on the roof, the younger son/sibling caught atop an outbuilding. The muddy waters churned and roiled with monstrous things. I hadn't put a face to these creatures yet.

"Johnny," I heard a small voice call from the darkness inside. I sighed and regretted letting him stay downstairs to watch *Phantasm* with me. Even after his countless promises of "*I won't be scared.*" We'd done this dance before.

"Yeah," I whispered back. A car drove around the bend, slowing to see what the hell this crazy boy was doing on his roof after midnight. This happened often.

"Are you coming in soon?" Roscoe whispered, that loud whisper that isn't really one at all. We were the only ones home, there was no need for whispers.

"In a bit. I'm writing. Why?"

"I don't like being alone in here."

"Don't be a dork. You're not alone. I'm right here. Literally less than ten feet away."

"But Mom isn't here. And what if something happens?"

"Nothing is going to happen. I'm right here, writing and watching you. You'll be okay, you're safe. Go to sleep."

"Nobody will be okay," he said, his voice was reedy, and he punctuated his statement with a heavy sigh.

"I'll be right in," I said, pulling the page from the machine and crawling in through the window. I cradled it like a baby, before reaching out to lift the typewriter back inside.

I sat it on the desk and walked over to the beds. Kneeling down, I pulled Roscoe's blanket up and told him to go to sleep again.

"Okay." He smiled, his eyes moist. "Thanks, Johnny."

He was snoring in no time as I sat at my desk, listening to Def Leppard through my headphones. The little red light on my stereo was a staring alien eye. I grabbed a pen, and I sat up straight.

"Nobody will be okay." I wrote in my idea notebook. I underlined it twice.

That simple statement made me very anxious. I stared out the window and watched the trees across the road. Their branches whispered in the breeze. Somewhere in the darkness, I heard cats fighting. That sound was exactly how my insides felt. Claws and screams.

I had no idea as to why.

- 3 -

RENNIE BENSON was a town fixture. A bit feeble of mind and not much to look at. Very round and witchy looking. Like *Broom Hilda* for real. She was usually stationed at the end of her porch, chain-smoking and muttering to herself. Rumors flew about her like bats. Rumors that some of the town's more affluent men would frequent her home for "entertainment" in the night. Rumors that grew all the more odd given her bizarre demise years later, on a day when they would find her in her trailer. Blood coated the walls and ceiling. Doors and windows were all locked from the inside. Details via the gossip chain ranged from she was cut into pieces to there was no body at all, just blood everywhere. The trailer would be dragged out to the dump where it would remain as a taunt to kids until it mysteriously burned, leaving a long, charred box on the clay like a shadow.

But none of that had happened yet.

Roscoe came into the kitchen with a paper grocery bag, which from the frantic scrabbling and movement, could only contain our cat Bandit. She loved to play in empty bags, though she did not so much love it when we would grab the bag and roll down the top to carry her around the house. No wonder that cat was crazy and mean.

"Where were you a while ago?" I asked him, "I called for you outside and you never answered. I was going to make you lunch. I have Oodles of Noodles."

"I was down the street with Mike." He dropped the bag and a burst of gray fur launched from it like a rocket, hissing as she darted.

"Have fun?" I asked as I turned on the burner and set to filling the pan with water.

"Sure. We walked over to Eggar's and bought some penny candy. Then we played He-Man. And then he walked part way home with me. Oh! And then Rennie Benson showed us her puppies." He beamed.

I stopped and looked at him. That woman unnerved me, always had, but I knew her to be relatively harmless.

"Puppies?" I asked. The burner hissed as I sloshed a little water over the side of the pan.

"Yep. She asked us if we wanted to see her puppies. We said sure. I like puppies." He stopped as though unsure he should continue. "So, we followed her into her trailer and she got them. They was in the freezer in a plastic bag. Tiny little puppies, there was four of them. They looked like they were asleep. She said that's how they were born. They were pink and snowy."

I had no response. It was such a fucked up thing, yet my little brother just informed me that a grown-up had trolled out dead frozen puppies she was keeping in her freezer to some little boys. I stirred the soup. "Um. I think you'd better not go around her anymore. Okay?"

"Okay. How come? She's nice and she looks like that witch from the *Bugs Bunny* cartoon."

"I can't really explain it. Just don't. And for God's sake don't tell Mom or Gram about the puppies."

He was in the room, watching *Starcade* before I finished that sentence. I swirled the spoon around and around and peered into the whirlpool it created. Sometimes real life is much weirder than anything a person could write or rent to watch.

- 4 -

WHEN GRAM stopped by the next morning to visit, she brought me the newspaper from the previous day. I immediately turned to page two and scoped the piddly little movie theater advertisement. The Clifton was the only theater around and it was forty-five minutes away. No *Jedi*. They were still running *WarGames*. I sighed and closed the paper and gave it back to Gram.

"Keep it for when you change the litter box," she said.

We were waiting for Roscoe to come down so we could help Gram deliver her Avon. I was not a fan of the activity, but I was a big fan of the pizza or ice cream that followed. I leaned into the living room and yelled up the stairs. "C'mon!"

"I can't find my shoes," Roscoe hollered back.

"They're down here, Dippy!" I baited as I bent to pick up the battered canvas sneakers that lay by the sofa.

"Shut up!" He screeched as he bounded down the steps.

Once at the bottom, he assumed his patented rhino stance. It was his main defense to my picking. He'd lean forward and ram me with his hard head. He charged, and I raised my knee. His face connected with my kneecap and he screamed as blood began to pour from his nose.

Sensing immediately that I was going to be in major trouble, I started whispering at him. "Shh. Shhh. Be quiet. It's okay. You're okay," as I pulled handfuls of Kleenex from the box and wiped his nose. It kept bleeding. I kept at it.

"What's going on in there?" Gram called from the kitchen, her gaze blotted out by the cloud of Marlboro smoke swirling around her.

"Nothing," I lied as Roscoe sat on the couch, head tilted back and I got the bleeding to stop. 'Don't tell or we won't get any pizza or ice cream," I threatened.

Ross sniffed and wiped his eyes. "I hate you," he said.

"You don't. Let's go," I snapped, not caring if it was true. Then.

By the time we stopped for pizza, Roscoe had all but forgotten I had nearly broken his nose. For the time being, anyway.

- 5 -

ANGELO WAS another denizen of our town. The story went that in the late seventies, he was a bright and promising student. Whip smart and so talented at painting and drawing, the school art teacher had created an apprenticeship sort of situation for him. The art teacher worked outside of his day school gig as a painter of motorcycles and vans—those epic busty barbarianesses and dragon scenes that rolled the highways at one time. That's what he dabbled in. Angelo would have been even better, but one day some assholes sprinkled PCP on his lunch or something and his brain fried. That's how the story always went—his brain fried. Like an egg or some scrapple. He lost the ability to speak coherently and all control of his motor functions and coordinative skills. He became a sort of palsied-mascot, a walking billboard for "*Just Say No.*" He walked everywhere, in a trademark shambling gait, with his spasming arms flailing like a crooked windmill. The story usually ended with the teacher being so distraught over the whole ordeal that he resigned and went on the road as a travelling biker tattooist.

One night, some kids broke into the Buy 'N Box, our local grocery store. They stole a little money and upon escaping into the alley, they saw a shadow. They yelled at the man to stop, but he kept walking. They chased him down, eventually catching him near the old railroad bridge at the end of town. It was poor Angelo, and the youths wrestled him to the ground, beat him to death with a rock, and then tossed him into the creek below. They thought he would be able to finger them or tell someone what he saw. They couldn't have been from the area or they would have known neither was a possibility. A few of the volunteer firemen pulled Angelo from the creek the next morning, pruned and white as linen.

There, under the bridge, had always been a prime spot for fishing. Usually teeming with bass and catfish. I swear, from the moment they pulled Angelo from that muddy water, the hole was scarred. Stained and ruined. All that was hauled out after that morning was catfish, but they weren't quite right. Small and fat and mushroom white, the cats caught there screamed and belched with an ungodly racket until they were thrown back. Even on the calmest day, the water never cleared. Always shadow-choked and murky. Once in a while someone would fish from that bridge, a tourist or visiting outsider. But most of us stopped fishing it all together.

- 6 -

THE MONTH of July went fast. Counted off in dozens of kickball games, Wiffle ball battles, bike riding adventures, and hours of horror movies played on enormous rental VHS player machines. Sweaty days of playing outside from sun up until sunset, bookended with films like *The Being, Scalps, Blood Beach*, and *The Boogens*. Gallons of Pepsi and barrels of Middleswarth BBQ potato chips kept us nourished. We were juggernauts, and we were tearing a hole in our world, one scabbed knee at a time. Paving the way with all the dirt we could carry under our fingernails.

We were still awaiting the arrival of *Jedi* but it had yet to materialize. Gram had recently gotten a satellite dish, which at that time was roughly the size of a small house. No exaggeration. This enormous thing that looked like something out of *Space: 1999* and stood taller than her trailer. It really didn't pull in that many more channels than her old antenna did. Still, I was thrilled we could get MTV. I would sit for an hour and eat my lunch while wallowing in the visual boon of videos by *Buggles, Wham!* and *Split Enz*.

My pap worked at a local military depot. I never really knew what he did, just that he went to work at two in the afternoon and came home later at night. He was a gruff man, a giant to me, well over six feet tall and no nonsense. I had always thought Roscoe was his favorite, as they acted like pals. *"My little Buddy"* was what he called my little brother, whereas I was just "Little Johnny." I always felt like he didn't understand me at all. I felt that way about a lot of folks in the town, hell, even in my family. I was not an athlete. I read books and wrote stories. I was lanky and had long hair. I loved horror and music. I was a self-made pariah. There always seemed to be an odd air of resentment and awkwardness between Pap and I. Then he got cancer. By the end of that summer, he weighed as much as Roscoe and passed away.

It hit me hard. It was my first close encounter with loss and the very grown-up feelings of regret and guilt. I had accused my grand-father of playing favorites that spring. I told him he loved Roscoe more than me. I pouted and never went out when he was there, until after he was bed bound. I went out to see him one time after that.

I was sitting on the sofa one August morning, putting on my boots for work. I had a summer job with the borough doing main-tenance work. I heard the phone ring and as I reached to pick it up, I heard Mom get it upstairs. Gently, I lifted the earpiece from the cradle and held a hand over the mouthpiece. I listened in.

"Karen." It was Gram, her voice a small sketch on thin tissue. Weak and fragile. "Pappy died. We had to take him to Lewistown Hospital early and he passed right when we got there." Gram sobbed. I closed my eyes and put the phone down. I silently wept for fifteen minutes and then went to work. I didn't know what else you were supposed to do. I was trying to be grown-up. Grown-ups just keep going, don't they?

I never really got to apologize. To tell him I was sorry and that I loved him and knew he loved me. I wish I could say I learned from this, but as life would roll on, this pattern of regret and guilt in the face of death would repeat itself. It's like tripping over the same step every day, knowing where it is and knowing you do it all the time but not being able to not do it.

I sat in the borough building and waited for my boss to arrive. I actually had two of them. They were both local volunteer fire-man. When they arrived and saw me sitting there on the couch, they looked shocked and uncomfortable. They didn't know I knew about my pap. They knew, because they were EMTs and had accompanied him on the run earlier. The younger man, Boodle, sat beside me and with as much tact and seriousness as he could mus-ter, broke the news of my grandfather's passing. I looked at him and used all my strength to not shed a tear. I was almost thirteen and still thought that wasn't something boys did.

"I know," I managed.

"Why are you here? Do you want me to take you home?" Old Joe asked from his perch on the cooler. The overlong ash on the end of his cigarette defied gravity. I felt like that ash. Defiant and smoldering.

"I guess." I stared at the green stains on my boots, the blood of a summer's worth of grass. "No. Thanks." The words sounded like a whisper in a quiet room. "I can walk. Thanks."

And with that I left the small building and its reek of grease and gasoline. I heard their voices fade until there was no sound save for the birds and the occasional blast of AC/DC or Hank Williams Jr. from a passing car. I walked the back alley and got home in time to see Gram pull in. Before she even got out of the car, I threw myself in her arms and broke down. "I'm sorry I said what I said to Pappy. I'm so sorry." I bawled.

"It's okay, Johnny. He knows. He knew." She stroked my hair and held me until I calmed down. And then we went in the house and went through it all again.

Often times, I still go through it.

- 7 -

THE NOTE asked me to walk down to the store and get a few things. Milk, bread, a package of hamburger, and two packs of Marlboro Lights. Atop the paper with my mother's painfully legible script were three Five Dollar Food Stamps and a five-dollar bill for the cigarettes. I sighed.

I hated going to the store with food stamps almost as much as I hated buying cigarettes. I resented having to bear the social awkwardness and embarrassment that went along with welfare. But it was necessary. Even with working three jobs, Mom made just enough to keep the house paid for and food in our bellies. Personally, I hated smoking. Both of my parents did it. My gram smoked like a fiend. And my pap had smoked as well, Camel unfiltered. I was not very vocal in my disdain of their habit; Roscoe handled that for me. He scolded and lectured and badgered them for it. The irony being that when we reached adulthood, Roscoe would be the one who took up smoking while I did not. Funny how that shit happens.

I sighed again and picked up the note and the money and stamps, crammed them into the pocket of my blue jean cut-offs, pulled on my Mötley Crüe shirt and slipped out the back door. Roscoe was watching cartoons and I didn't want him to hear me and want to tag along. Sometimes, a quiet walk is essential for a brooding young man.

- 8 -

AUGUST SAUNTERED over the hill one day, cocky and cool. On her heels were the hallmarks of the end of summer. The whisper of cornstalks in the fields. The Homecoming Carnival. Hot days and almost chilly nights. A hint of autumn on the air, with its slight graveyard dirt and cinnamon taste. The carnival was something the whole town looked forward to. It was actually the Fireman's Carnival but had long been referred to as "The Homecoming" because it was a time when folks who had long ago moved away from town would return to visit with friends and family, catching up over funnel cake and french fries. Conversations and candy apples. Greasy burgers from the fireman's food stand. There were a half dozen shoddy rides and lots of game stands where children wasted dollars like toilet tissue. It was exciting and everything a child could hope for.

I wasn't near the midway when the Ferris wheel fell over; I was over by the grand stand watching the local hard rock band, *Knipshun*, set up. One minute their guitarist was laying cable and setting up amps, the next, a tidal wave of screams washed over the buildings and we were assaulted with terror and chaos.

Luckily, there was no one on the ride at the time. The wheel runner had just started the ride to do a few turns when there was a terrible groan and the giant metal eye tilted. A loud snap and some sparks lead to the tilt turning to a fall which ended in a huge crash as it toppled onto the Ring Toss game and the one where you throw the ping pong balls into the little fish bowls. No one was killed. There was only one injury—the guy who ran the Ring Toss. He broke an arm diving to push a few children back and out of the way. The Ferris wheel was history, the game stand was too. And roughly two dozen goldfish lost their lives in the tragedy. An investigation would find nothing wrong with the wheel, in design or assembly. They would never know why it fell. The carnival still limps into town yearly, but they've never had another Ferris wheel.

I often think back to that event and how it could have been so much worse. There could have been a dozen children on the wheel when it went down. It could have fallen over the other way and landed on the merry-go-round and its long line of toddlers. I also look at it as just a punctuation mark. An emphasis of a fact. Nothing is stable and all things are not guaranteed to be what we expect. As a kid, that is something you never think on and often times, even well into adulthood. But it is a hard and painful lesson to learn when you do. One that usually leaves pale white marks on the skin and raw red welts on the soul.

PART III

AUGUST AND EVERYTHING AFTER

- 1 -

I STOOD on the front porch and took in the cool morning. There was a thin veil of fog coiled around the bushes and trees, and the birds were silent. The huge white water tank stood on the hill across from our house. Like a tumor. The mist caressed it like ancient fingers. All was quiet. Eerily so.

I stood in my red pajama pants and a threadbare Haunted River t-shirt and shivered. I heard the sound of an engine and watched the bend until I saw old man Price take the curve in his mustard yellow pickup. He passed and raised a hand in greeting. He seemed to be driving in slow motion. It was almost like he was not a part of the live scene, but somehow older footage that was superimposed over the current frame. It made my nerves jangle and my head ache a little. I waited until he disappeared from view, and then I turned and went back in the house, the tang of his exhaust still haunting my nose.

I sat at the table and nursed my tea, nibbled my toast, and unfolded yesterday's paper that Gram had brought in. This was my favorite part of the day. The hour or so between my waking up and Roscoe waking up, I relished the alone time and quiet. I took another gulp of my tea and opened the paper. After checking the theater ad and noting that *Jedi* was due next week, I scanned the crime log and the obituaries. Once I read the death notice for Henry Price, I closed the paper and shook my head. He had apparently died early yesterday morning, working in his barn. Heart attack or stroke. I had just waved at him less than a half an hour before. He had waved back. My headache slammed back and my stomach shivered. I threw my other piece of toast in the trash and went back to bed.

[This sort of thing seemed to happen often when I was growing up. In fact, it was not but maybe five years later that Mike, Roscoe's friend, would tell me a very similar tale. He claims that he was sitting in the pew at the Nazarene church, waiting for his gram. He did this every Sunday. And this week she was late. Mike waited and waited and eventually was committed to the sermon as he didn't want the attention he'd garner trying to sneak out. After church, his gram called and said, "Mike, sorry I missed church but your Uncle George passed away."

Mike said, "What?! He looked fine when I saw him at church this morning, sitting there in his suit singing and smiling."

There was a pause and then his gram replied, "Mike, George died last night."

Mike swears it to be true and given my own experiences with Mr. Price, I don't doubt it. You grow up with people your whole life, small towns especially. The people and the place become part of your very fiber. And sometimes, I think the weave may be a bit too strong.]

●●●

WHEN I got up for the day, for the second time, it was raining. A nice steady rain. The air was cool and smelled of water and grass and worms. I sat at my desk and watched it, the rain. Closed my eyes and could still see it. Roscoe was downstairs watching TV. I could hear him laughing. *Tom & Jerry.* I grabbed a shirt and a pair of cut off shorts from the pile of clothing on the floor. It was my Pat Benatar shirt. I smelled it and took it with me into the bathroom. I stood under the hot water and closed my eyes tight. So tight I could hear the blood in my head. It thrummed and howled. I thought about this summer. The weird things. The sad things. The bad things and the good things. I thought about Mom and wondered if she'd ever be truly happy. Thought about Roscoe and how one day we'd be living apart, about how I was practically a parent to him for these last few years and one day I'd be gone, living somewhere with my own family. Would it hurt him like it did when Dad left? Would he be happy? Would he ever really forgive me? I opened my eyes and rinsed the shampoo from my hair.

"I gotta go!" Roscoe's voice cut through my cocoon of steam and suds. I ignored him.

"Johnny!" he yowled, and I sighed.

"Go upstairs and go. I'm not done." I reached out to pull the accordion door closed. Our house only had a shower in the tiny half-bath, downstairs. The real bathroom was upstairs but featured only a large clawed tub.

"Mom's in there," he shouted.

"Tough tits. You'll have to hold it a few minutes. I'm almost done."

I finished rinsing and then grabbed my towel and dried off. I barely got dressed and out of the tiny room before Roscoe bounded in like his ass was on fire, not even bothering to pull the door shut before emptying his bladder. Outside the rain kept coming down.

- 2 -

THE MAN hung in the tree like Christ. Not quite holy, though. He was stripped to the waist, his already baggy jeans, saggy and soggy from the rain. A frayed length of rope cinched them around a skeletal waist.

Jimmy, Tommy, Mike, Roscoe, and I just stood there looking up. We had been heading down to the creek, to the Old House to play. The Old House was an abandoned shack; it was a squat thing that sat on the bank of the creek. It looked like a big old face. It was wildly cool. A few trees had grown up through the floor boards and found their way out via the ceiling. Inside, was old moldering furniture and pictures on the walls. No one had ever said who lived there or why they left, why it was turned over to the stern fists of nature for pummeling. All we knew was it was a cool place to hang out and plot world domination. The overwhelming amount of empty beer cans and cigarette butts let us know we weren't alone in that sentiment. There were also a few water-marked magazines with naked ladies in them on the floor.

But on this day, we didn't make it to the Old House. We were about fifty yards down the path, almost to the junction where our lower acre succumbed to thick brush and shoulder high weeds and became one with the forest. That was when Roscoe stopped and looked up and made a short, odd noise. A cross between a gasp and a hiccup. I recognized his terror mask immediately, from the cow incident earlier that summer.

"Roscoe," I called, as I looked up and saw what was the matter. My mind could not stitch together anything coherent to say.

The man had obviously been there a while. He would have been invisible from anywhere else but where we were, which was directly below. He was about fifteen feet up. His hands were secured to the branches with rope, the same that held up his jeans. His palms were turned upward and filled with weeds and grass. He had ribbons laced around his fingers—red, white, and blue. He wore no shirt. His skin was mottled and gray and glistened like mushroom flesh. It had sunken and pulled taut and looked like some sort of rubber. There was a hole in his chest, not like he was shot or anything, just a big hole. The size of a bowling ball, the flesh and skin pulled back from the edges and pinned to the body with granny pins (the kind that are long and have the little plastic beads on the end). Where his heart had lived was now a nest, dead grass and twigs and bits of paper peeking from the wound. When the crow flew from within, we all screamed. Roscoe ran back towards the house as fast as his stubby legs could go. The rest of us stayed and kept looking.

There was a swatch of cloth tied around his eyes. It was red, a bandana. Another piece of rope snaked around the trunk and across his open mouth, tied in a thick knot at the side. His teeth were startlingly white in contrast to the shade of the woods and the gray glisten of his lips around them. The ants that crawled on the teeth stood out like black stars in a white sky. His long hair (it may not have been long, just looked it given the sallow skullish look of the face and head) hung over his forehead. There was a large cut across the middle of his crooked (broken) nose, like a smaller second mouth. His feet were bare and there was more ribbon wrapped around his toes. At the base of the tree was a pair of work boots; they were standing on top of a cigar box.

Mike moved the boots and picked up the box.

"Don't," whispered Tommy. "That's evidence."

"I'll put it back." Mike undid the latch and lifted the lid. His brow furrowed, wavy lines as though he were a cartoon. He held the box out towards us, showing the contents. He shrugged. It was empty save for four things: a worn silver dollar, a pocket knife, a playing card—the seven of diamonds, and a rabbit's foot with the little ball chain for keys, like those won in carnivals. It might have once been dyed red or purple. It had seen and been kissed by flame, singed down to the mummified bone and flesh. I gasped as it reminded me of something personal. Something sad and special. Mike closed the box and put it back.

[My Uncle Roebuck had died when my dad was a small boy— that being said, it's obvious I never knew the man. My nanny used to tell stories about him and my other uncles when I would spend time with her. A lovely woman with smiling eyes, even when she told you stories that chilled the blood or cracked your heart. Like the one where she encountered a spirit in the shape of a black cat with a baby's face. So many stories.

But this one goes like this: My Uncle Roe was a truck driver along with my Uncle Chuck. They both worked for the same out-fit and if my memory hasn't marred the story, one weekend, my Uncle Chuck had a date. He was also scheduled to work. He was to haul a trailer full of steel pipe and rod. He eventually convinced Roe to take the load so he could keep his date. He'd make it up to him somehow later.

That night it rained, and Uncle Roe wrecked the rig. Eight tons of steel rod punched up through the cab and erased him from it. My Uncle Chuck never fully recovered or forgave himself. I believe there was a grieving guilt-ridden shadow on his back from that night until the heart attack took him some forty years later.

My nanny had Roe's keychain in a carnival glass candy dish on her mantel. It was a rabbit's foot, dyed orange and crisped by fire. When she'd tell the awful story of his death, she'd always get it out to show me. When I saw the contents of that damn box that day, it truly shook me. There is no way that could have been any sort of coincidence. I never had anything to prove otherwise, but I know in my heart, it was a statement...by who or what I'm unsure.]

We all just stood and looked up and no one said a word. Not when the clouds began to frown and blacken. Not when the first rumbles and grumbles of thunder sounded, and not even when the first fat raindrops began to snap and thump through the trees. We just looked up and let our eyes fill with rain.

- 3 -

I WANTED Gram to give me more quarters for the jukebox. She wouldn't. She didn't want to hear "It's Raining Again" by Supertramp or "The Devil Went Down to Georgia" anymore. The last only being repeated because it was the *son-of-a-bitch* version. So, we sat, eating our pizza while Olivia Newton John asked us to get physical. They really needed to update that jukebox; the songs were from three years prior. Roscoe was playing with his cheese, and I had eaten all my pizza and drunk two glasses of soda, belching the alphabet. Gram was frowning, then smiling and shaking her head.

"Johnny, don't be a pig," she said.

"Excuse me," I mumbled, insincerely.

"Did the cops say who the man was? The Tree Scarecrow?" I asked as I crunched a mouthful of ice from my empty cup. I had been following the story in the three-page tragedy known as the local paper. No one knew the man's identity. Why he was in the tree. There were no clues, just a bunch of odd stuff. The cave in his chest was filled with grass and shredded money for the crows to nest in. Yeah, they found shredded money in there. The man's stomach was apparently full of dimes and pennies, Mercury Head dimes and wheat pennies. That was all condensed into a two-paragraph-long travesty that nuzzled between the rash of brush fires in Saltine Borough and the stolen tractor tires from out at Newman's farm in Dogtree.

"No. Not anyone from around here." She stuck a cigarette in her mouth and lit it with her Bic. Drag. Exhale. Smoke in my face and food. "They have no idea who he was." Pause. Drag. Exhale. "Think he may've done it to himself. Just tied himself up there to die." She coughed, and it sounded painful and moist.

"And then put a big hole in his chest for the birds to nest in?" I asked, a little snarkier than I intended.

"I don't know. Just finish your food. I want to finish the Avon before it gets dark." She rummaged through her huge purse for her wallet and gave me a twenty to go pay the bill. Roscoe wiped his cheesy fingers on the tablecloth as I walked away. I felt all eyes as I went to the counter. They all turned away as I went back to the table. It was almost mechanical.

- 4 -

WE STAYED the night at Gram's. She lived in a ancient trailer with a crazy cat lady amount of pets. Dogs and cats. I wouldn't realize until I was much older and lived away from it for a while just how gross and unacceptable those conditions were, but she was happy while there and that seemed to be enough. It was windy, and I sat on the couch watching Lawrence Welk. I didn't like that show, not one bit, but it was the show that preceded *Hee-Haw*, which I did like. Gram only got one channel and even that depended on the cooperation of the fates and Mother Nature. Often times I had to don my gram's pink flip-flops and make my way to the side of the trailer and hand-turn the antenna, rust coming off onto my wet hands. But if it meant I got to see Roy Clark play that banjo clearly, that was enough for me. She had given up on her satellite dish and had it disconnected.

"I ain't paying all that money just to get maybe four more channels than the one I always could get," she reasoned.

They interrupted Welk for a local news bulletin. The police in Chambersburg had arrested a man in connection to some robberies and he confessed to the bizarre murder of the man in the tree. The footage of the arrest was jumpy and frantic, but it was easy to raise one's eyebrows at. The man had confessed to beating and killing a man. Force feeding him small change and hollowing out his chest for a bird house. Climbing a tree to display the corpse nearly twenty feet above ground, the man who claimed to be responsible for this act was being wheeled into the courthouse. In a wheelchair. Because he had no legs. No fucking legs.

I just looked at Gram, but she was on the phone with Margie. When I looked back at the TV, the news bulletin had given way to a commercial with Loretta Lynn showing me her delicious looking chicken she made with Crisco. I waited through twelve more minutes until *Hee-Haw* started, all seven-hundred and twenty seconds spent thinking about the man in the tree and the legless man who said he did it but didn't.

PART IV

THE SKY CRIES MURDER

- 1 -

I STOOD and waited for my turn on the *Galaga* machine at the Minit-Mart. Tony was hogging the machine and had been for over an hour. His strategy was simple. He'd break wind. Most of the time his fetid fart cloud would scatter the kids that crowded and whined for their go at the machine. Sometimes it wouldn't work. I stood there, nose pinched between my thumb and forefinger, and waited.

"Hurry up, you asshole," I said, sounding a bit like a Muppet.

"I'm almost done," Tony assured, as he shifted his weight to one foot and lifted his leg. I turned my head as he let it rip.

The cowbell tied to the door sounded as a gaggle of teenagers entered. All with matching dirty jeans, snuff rings proud on the back pockets. The oldest—I only knew his last name was Kreider—was at the counter buying cigarettes. I could hear the music that was wafting from their pickup in the parking lot, even though the windows were closed and the store's sounds were competing. It was Iron Maiden. I watched through the dirty glass, the old farmers and ladies at the gas pumps, their dagger looks following from the noisy truck to the store. The kids paid for their stuff and left. I watched as they sauntered across the asphalt. Their boots scuffed and thudded. And though the sun was above them and the heat lines shimmered over the hot ground, they cast no shadows. They got in the truck and drove off. I seemed to remember it as a truck I saw in the paper as wrecked last spring.

I would have thought more on the subject, were it not finally my turn at *Galaga*. And my chance to swaddle Tony in my own stink clouds.

- 2 -

DINNER WAS spaghetti. It was often spaghetti. I sat at the table eating mine while Roscoe sat across from me twirling his around his fork, picking out the chunks of onion and grinning with sauce all over his face like a drunken clown. Mom was upstairs getting ready for her shift. I looked at the money on the counter. Five bucks. A small fortune to go to Joe's Video and rent something to watch. I decided it would be a John Carpenter night and planned to rent *Escape From New York* and *The Fog*. Possibly *Christine*. Mom swooped into the kitchen and straightened her scrub top. She took a gulp from her cold coffee and sat the mug in the sink.

"You boys know the rules," she said.

We nodded our head with our mouths still full and she smiled.

"Good. I left you money for some movies. You may only walk to Joe's and back. No running around town or anything. I'll call and check."

She gave a stern look we knew was bullshit. We never wandered town after she left, but she had never actually called to make certain. She gave Roscoe a side hug, so as to not get sauce on her whites. She hugged me and spoke softly into my ear.

"Be good. Doors locked as soon as you get in. It's different now."

She picked up her cigarette case from the counter and slung her purse over her shoulder. "Love you guys," she called as we heard the back door close.

I frowned a little, thinking of how dire her parting words had seemed. I looked at Roscoe. He was busy shaking parmesan cheese down his throat. I shook my head and finished my plate. The night continued as planned.

- 3 -

TOMMY, MIKE, Roscoe, and I sat and watched Wile E. Coyote building another trap that was destined to fail. Roscoe and Mike were laying on the floor, closest to the television. Tommy and I were sitting on the couch, talking low.

"So, you saw that news thing on Saturday night?" Tommy asked.

I stole a glance to make sure the kids weren't listening. "Yeah. Fucked up, huh?"

Tommy picked up the albums from the cushion beside him and laid them on the coffee table. "How the hell did that dude do it, then? He had no legs!"

Tommy was wound up as usual. He had initially knocked on our door at nine o'clock with the new Twisted Sister and Judas Priest albums in hand. We planned to play them and then go walk the town.

"My mom and dad were talking, I heard them say the legless man's prints were on stuff. The boots, the box, and the shit inside." Tommy got all the best gossip by eavesdropping on his parents and spoke so fast that most people couldn't decipher anything he said.

I shook my head and pulled a sliver of the fake veneer from the corner of the table before I replied. "That makes no sense. They still don't know who the dead guy is. Why the guy made him into a birdhouse or why he fed him money and shit. So bizarre."

Roscoe and Mike burst into laughter and I looked up in time to see Coyote walking across the desert looking like an accordion.

"There's been a lot of that this summer," I added.

Tommy smiled and stood, grabbing the albums from the table. "Let's go listen to these. The Priest is killer." And the boys began to laugh again as Tommy and I went upstairs to rock out.

"Did you see *Jedi* yet?" Tommy asked as Halford screeched in the background.

"No, hasn't come around yet."

I knew where this was going. Though Tommy was my best friend, he was a bit of a bragger and always had and did shit first. I knew what was coming before he spoke.

"I saw it two weeks ago. When I was in Florida visiting my gram."

I sighed and waited for him to begin his long-detailed spoil of the movie. There was a loud pound on the door and it opened enough for my mother, looking like hell as she peered in.

"Johnny! You know I worked all night. Turn that down or use your headphones!" She pulled the door closed, hard. I turned the volume down and shrugged at Tommy, who luckily forgot what he was about to say as he began talking about how his mom was taking him to Philly to catch David Bowie in a few weeks. Sometimes, the scales of our friendship, or at least how I perceived it, tilted towards the hate side of things. I suspect the weight was skewed by the thin fingers of jealousy.

- 4 -

HOURS LATER, Tommy had left and Roscoe was sleeping in the bottom bunk. Mom was working. It was quiet. I sat at my desk with the lights off. Arms crossed and head resting upon them. The window behind the desk was open, and I watched the woods across the road. Listened to the hum of the lone streetlight in front of the house, the streetlight that announced *"You are leaving this sad little town!"* unless you were coming the other direction, then it was *"Welcome to this sad affair."*

It made the darkness more of a bright brown, and so I sat there in the dark watching the lighter dark. Shadows moved there. They lumbered and cavorted. I couldn't make out what they were, but they were tall and thin. Limbs snaked and danced against the gray painted sides of the water tower that stood on the small swell of a hill. Like shadows on a movie screen. My teeth found my bottom lip and grabbed hold. I sat and stared and didn't move a muscle. The shadows played on for another hour. That's when the big lumber truck rolled around the bend and into town and obscured my view for a few seconds. Once the gears finished groaning and it lurched down the hill into town, I looked back to the tower and the dancing shadows. They were gone, if they were ever there at all. I slowly pulled the window down and turned the catch. I drew the curtains all but a sliver that was lined up with the pillow end of the top bunk. I climbed up and nestled beneath the sheet and blanket. Epiphany grumbled and settled back to her slumber. I laid there on my side, peering through the crack in the curtains at the hillside where those strange things romped less than a half an hour ago. I hoped I'd see them coming, if they decided to do so.

Below me, Roscoe slept and slept and slept.

- 5 -

WE WERE sitting in the car waiting for Gram. She was taking us to visit our other grandmother, Nanny, but we had to stop at the bank first. I opted to wait in the car, which then meant Roscoe was waiting in the car and I was to keep an eye on him. He was sitting in the back, jabbering about who knows what, while I sat in the front, watching the street behind the security of my sunglasses. People are curious all the time, but especially when being watched unaware. Their natural faces show, devoid of the masks they save for public interaction or politeness.

I watched Mr. Gunnells as he set up the outside items in front of the hardware store. Standing the rakes, shovels, and hoes in their rack. His lightly tanned brow was furrowed like a farmer's field. His mouth, a wrinkle in a leather pouch. He stopped periodically to move his glasses further up his nose.

Walking in his direction was Mrs. Crates. Almost as wide as she was tall, but the friendliest woman in town. I always found her pleasantry intriguing given that her husband was one of the most miserable fuckers I had ever encountered, and this could and would be corroborated by ninety percent of the populace. He was mean and yelled and supposedly hit her. But she faced the town daily, cloaked in garish makeup and bright clothes and a huge smile on her gaudy lips. She laced every interaction with enough *honeys* and *sweeties* to pacify a diabetic. She was admirable in her own pathetic way.

I heard Gram's smoker cough, followed by her loud voice, and turned to see her standing at the end of the car. She was talking to Old Man Runk. I couldn't hear much of their conversation but I knew it must pertain to something about the body or us, as she turned around and nodded towards the car, their voices swung into a lower gear. I stopped watching and sunk into the seat, sliding the cotton pads of the headphones over my ears, but didn't turn it on lest Night Ranger prevent me from hearing about the death of the legless man. About his bizarre suicide in the Chambersburg county jail. About how the man with no lower limbs somehow managed to set himself on fire in an empty cell with nothing but a cot, mattress, and wall-mounted toilet. And most curiously, how the fire had been so fierce that his shadow had been burned into the wall. About the fact that the shadow had its legs.

- 6 -

IN THE side yard, we had a copse of trees. In one of them, we had attempted to build a tree house at one point. In reality, it was about six boards nailed across two large branches, a bench in the top of the tree. A place where we could sit and just think and watch the road that passed the front of the house. It was cool. I read countless *Fangoria* magazines up there. One time, Roscoe climbed up there and dozed off. I might have climbed up and nailed the tail of his shirt to the boards. School would be starting in two weeks, all that we'd looked forward to, gone like so many dreams. If wishes were lies, they'd linger forever. I had been having a hard time that week. I was still quite agonized over my grandfather's death and the guilt I felt over the way I had acted. I felt like a bastard and didn't really want to be around anyone. I stayed in my room and stayed up all night watching HBO or writing. Growing up was a shitty thing to do to someone.

It was a cloudy day, cool, as the tongue of autumn was beginning to touch the days. I went outside and I climbed the tree, with a worn-out paperback of Richard Lewis' *The Spiders* that I had borrowed from my aunt. I reached the top and there upon the boards was a small piece of brown paper. The kind grocery store bags were made of. On it was one sentence, written in black marker. I did not recognize the writing, or maybe I did but I couldn't bring myself to think about it. I could not say the same for the message:

"~~Nobody~~ will be okay."

The thick line drawn through the word *Nobody* changed everything. Sometimes a little excision is all that is needed.

Lying atop the paper, acting as weight to keep the wind from taking it, was a silver dollar. It was an old Liberty Head silver dollar. Its face was worn smooth by a thousand thumb caresses. The back looked the same. I gasped and felt my eyes widen. This had belonged to my grandfather. It had been given to him by his father, shortly before he was killed in a logging accident. I had always looked at it when we stayed out at Gram's, always wished it were mine. I had memorized its eroded surface, the barely legible date stamped on the front. The tiny speck of blue paint that marked the edge. It was the same coin. I slipped it into my flannel shirt pocket along with the note and climbed back down from the perch. I no longer felt like reading. I felt a little nervous, slightly unsettled, and a lot forgiven. When I reached the bottom, Gram was pulling in to the driveway. I decided to keep the coin business to myself. A special marble in the pouch of my soul.

Instead, I ran over to ask her if she would take Roscoe and I to see *Jedi* on Saturday. It was finally here.

- 7 -

IT WAS Thursday. The days were crawling at a snail's pace, most likely due to the exciting prospect of finally seeing *Return of the Jedi* on Saturday. Gram wasn't going to take us; Mom had requested the night off, and we were indulging in a rare family night out. I couldn't wait. I was in the upstairs bathroom when I heard Roscoe yelling in the yard below. I walked over to the open window and looked out through the dirty screen. I ignored the husks of bees and flies laying in mounds that looked nearly ceremonial, between the screen and the outer sill.

"Shut up!" I yelled. The boy walked backwards across the yard with his hand flattened over his eyes, shielding his upward gaze from the sun.

"You shut up, Johnny!" he countered.

"What are you yammering about?" I asked.

"Kris is fighting with Tippy. They made Cherokee run across the road, and he could've gotten hit by a car!" Roscoe shouted. His red cheeks gave away his agitation.

I almost yelled back before catching myself. My little brother was upset because the ghosts of two dead dogs were quibbling and scared the ghost of a cat in to the street where he was worried it would be killed...again. I looked down and smiled. "Cherokee is okay. Go play out back."

Roscoe nodded and ran around to the backyard. I heard him calling for the dogs to follow, and I went back to the mirror. I leaned in close and rekindled my war on that damn pimple.

Later that afternoon, Roscoe and I indulged in one of our favorite past times. I fondly recall them as "Things that seemed like good ideas at the time of conception, but in execution..." At the foot of the hill by our house, we built a ramp. Hardly a wonder of engineering; it was basically a board leaned on a cinder block. At the top of this hill, I sat on my ten-speed bike. More of the Pee-Wee Herman style than the curled handle bar kind. Behind me, Roscoe stood on his skateboard and held onto the piece of clothesline that was tied to the bar that held the bicycle seat. He wrapped it around his wrists and held on tight as I looked back over my shoulder and said, "Here we go." The houses blurred by. I whooped and Roscoe yelled, and we whizzed down the hill going what seemed like a hundred miles an hour.

I hit the ramp just a hair off center. The board flipped over as the tire hit the brick, and the body of the bicycle swung sideways. I was prone on the asphalt, rolling to the edge, holding my skinned knees and swearing as Roscoe hit the bike, and then the brick, on his skateboard. He flipped over both like some sort of acrobat, but with none of the grace, and he rolled. Sadly, his strategy involved him dragging the bicycle along behind him as they were still connected by rope. The bike pedal had caught in one of the cinder block holes, so that was also coming along. I laid there bleeding and angry but laughing at the ridiculous sight of the little boy sideways across his skateboard, still rolling down the hill with a brick and a bicycle with a newly bent frame in tow. They all stopped when he hit the gravel of the parking lot at the garage below. I limped down as quickly as I could and untied him from the bike.

"You okay?" I asked him, awaiting the slaps and sobs.

He stood up and held his bleeding elbow, brushed the dirt and blood from his left knee and looked up at me. Through the tears and snot that covered his face, a smile broke through. "We should do it again," is what he said.

I dragged the brick out of the street and picked up the sad carcass of my bike. Roscoe grabbed his board and we shambled up the hill towards the house like something out of *Night of The Living Dead*.

That night, after we ate our sloppy joes and watched *The Sentinel*, I went down into the cellar to get the laundry from the dryer and bring it up for folding. I did so fairly quietly, and carried the basket into the dining room, a room we never allowed to live up to its name. Instead, we used the table that resided there to hold folded laundry and old newspapers. Boxes of stuff and books. I sat the basket on a chair and began folding my shirts. In the living room, Roscoe slept on the floor. The television was turned down, but I could see the screen from where I stood. On it, Abbott & Costello were being chased by a mummy. I'd seen it a million times. I saw headlights turn at the top of our hill. They washed through the drapes and across my arm. I stopped and went to the back room to peer out like Gladys Kravitz.

It was an old station wagon. It was gray with fins, making it look like some giant fish. It had the same washed-out photograph look that Price's truck had that morning. My stomach began to roll. I watched the car creep down the hill and turn into the parking lot of the old welding shop at the foot of our property. I could still see the cinder block sitting near the edge of the road where I'd left it. A very tall man got out and walked to the soda machine that stood guard at the front. I heard change drop, the sound carrying through the window screens as there was no competition from the night noises. The can *thunked* down and the man grabbed it with a long-fingered hand. I mean, *long.* Seeing it against the lighted building made me think of the vampire in *Nosferatu.* So long and spidery. He pulled the tab and tossed it into the weeds, then tilted back his head. His long neck bulged as he gulped down the contents. With one hand, he crushed the can into a small wad. Almost like balling paper. He tossed it into his mouth and I watched the throat constrict and squirm like a snake belly. He turned and looked up at the house, at the curtained window I peered through. At me. I could feel it. He pointed one of those fingers in my direction and smiled a very, very large smile.

"It's okay. Just thirsty," he called, but I got the feeling only I could hear. Then he walked back to the car. Moths and mosquitoes flitted and dive-bombed him as he stood by the vehicle. I heard the hiss and spark as they made contact with him, his coat and flesh acting like a bug lamp. He crawled in and pulled the door closed.

Slowly, he pulled back out in to the street, and disappeared around the corner.

Dogs began to howl and bark. I just stood there, all gooseflesh and chilled. My fidgety fingers unlocked the door and locked it again, just to be sure it was done. I turned off all the lights and sat in the dark next to my sleeping brother with the sharpest knife we owned on the floor next to me.

That is exactly how we were when Mom came home in the morning. We were grounded from watching scary movies when she worked for two weeks after that, which was all that remained of summer. To this day, I'm not sure I'm willing to swear it was real.

- 8 -

I WAS up with the sun on Saturday. I was sitting on the couch watching *Super Friends* when Roscoe came down.

"Johnny!" He squealed and jumped onto the sagging cushion next to me.

"Yes," I said with an exaggerated pause and a smile.

"It's *Jedi* Day!"

He stood up and jumped on the couch. The springs groaned, letting us know this was far from a wise activity. Roscoe kept at it, until we heard the crack, followed by a splintering sound, and Roscoe's legs and the cushion they stood upon dropped about ten inches to rest on the floor. I left my seat like I was on fire and stood motionless, waiting for the angry yell from upstairs. *"What are you guys doing?"*

We stood like stone.

Nothing.

[A lot of it most likely had to do with sleep deprivation, but our mom was not always known for her rationality. One time,

when Roscoe was about thirteen, I was picking on him. We were ascending the back steps to the house and I was egging him on, winding him up, and said something especially fuse-igniting as I entered the house. I then quickly turned and saw him rearing back to punch me. I pushed the door closed in time to protect my face but not to give him enough time to stop the swing. Roscoe's fist crashed through the window, cutting his knuckles and further infuriating him. I opened the door and he came in like a swarm bent on pummeling me.

Mom was in the kitchen and broke it up. She started spanking my brother while yelling, "I'm not beating you because you broke that window; I'm punishing you because you tried to hit your brother."

Roscoe countered, "He was picking on me. He said I was—(I have no idea what I said anymore) and so I tried to hit him and he shut the door before I could stop punching."

Mom paused in her fervent spanking and said, "Well, how the hell am I supposed to pay for that window?"

Her punishments were always somewhat humorous. I mean, we knew when we got her mad enough to hit, we'd done it, and we usually took the swats and the lesson they ingrained, but sometimes the hilarity won over. I made her so mad one time she hit me with a He-Man action figure. How can you not laugh at that?

But she did the best she could with two young boys, with not a lot of time at home, while putting her dreams of college and all that on hold to start a family that fell apart and left her having to work multiple jobs just to take care of us. These are things you don't consider while you're young. I used to be bitter of the time I spent cleaning the house, but no matter how bitter I was then, it was nothing compared to the guilt this woman shackled herself to. Looking back on things from adulthood is a sad and eye-opening thing. Always.]

Roscoe cried, quietly. "Mom's gonna be mad. She's not gonna take us to the movies," he managed at a low frantic pitch, with tears and snot marring his round face.

"Shh!" I hissed. "Get out of there."

He did. I pulled out the cushion and looked at the torn fabric covering the springs, which weren't bent or anything. The cross board had cracked under Roscoe's jumping and that was the only real damage. I stared for a moment and then had an idea.

The hammer hung from my belt loop as I climbed the tree. The handle thumped from my hip with each movement. I got to the top and climbed onto the planks that acted as our tree bench. I eased the claw end of the hammer beneath the head of the nail on the board closest to the trunk of the tree and pulled it free. I put the sap sticky thing in my pocket and removed the other three nails. I lifted the board free and tossed it backwards over the branches and bushes. I heard it hit the ground without looking back. After climbing down, I grabbed the board and went back in the house.

Inside, I placed the two-by-four across the frame under the cushions. It fit perfectly. I then pulled the torn cover fabric back over the wood and replaced the cushions as they should have been. I sat on the couch and wiggled around a bit; it held. It would work. All was well. For now. Roscoe was lying on the floor watching *Smurfs* and I picked up my book and went back to reading. The day rolled on.

- 9 -

WE GOT to the theater around seven o'clock. The movie started at seven-thirty. The line already stretched down the block. I was so excited I couldn't stand it. I think by this point in our lives we had only been to the movies a handful of times. We patiently made our way to the window and Mom got our tickets. She splurged for popcorn and didn't even make her sad *"we can't afford this face"* even though I am certain, under the skin, that was the expression. We went inside and took our seats. It smelled of melted butter, burnt popcorn and spilled soda—in other words, heavenly.

I sat on the end and looked over at my mother. She was only in her thirties, but the worry was etched on her face. She didn't look old per se, just tired. Very tired. I hoped she would not always have to work like she did. I hoped someday I could be a big writer or something and save her. I would do that. It's what sons do, I thought. I looked over at Roscoe, shoving buttery fistfuls of popcorn into his grinning mouth. I hoped he would grow up and be as happy as he was now. I hoped we would always be as close as we were at that moment. When one is young, dreams are reality in the waiting. It just seems so easy to assume things will play out a certain way. Then you grow and life gets stern and the learning gets harder and leaves bruises.

Sitting in the dark, waiting to watch some serious space-set coolness, we were a family.

The lights went out and the music began. My chest jumped with the sound. I took my mother's bony and calloused hand and held it. She looked over and smiled, an actual smile. A few minutes later, I let go of it.

It was the last time I wasn't too big to hold her hand. This is something that should never happen, but that realization was lost in the torrent of light sabers, Sarlacc pits, and Ewoks. By the end of the night, all I could remember was Carrie Fisher in that gold bikini. When the movie ended, we walked the two blocks to the lot where we parked. Roscoe dozed off within minutes of starting for home. Mom and I talked for the remaining half hour of the drive. It was the first of many adult conversations we would have. We talked about books and things. It was exciting and sad at the same time. Just like growing up. Just like living. Just knowing that it would eventually fade like an old Polaroid. Or a favorite concert t-shirt.

Just like everything does.

POSSESSED BY A
BROKEN WINDOW

MY FINGERTIP is getting raw from tracing the upholstery pattern on the arm of this damned chair, endless curlicues and swirls eroding pale skin to angry pink.

I've been sitting here for at least six hours or more a day, for the last three months. Actually, it's been the same month three times. I'll get to that. Maybe. I hear the squeak of nurse shoes in the hall like fleeing mice. I look up at the entrance and wait for her to come in. She will be holding a clipboard in her left hand, tight against her hip. Her eyes will be evasive, and she will still carry the smell of the cigarette she just smoked out in the courtyard. Her voice will be a shriveled thing. She enters as I just described, and I close my eyes and hear the replay in self-imposed blackout. Disembodied voices volley through the darkness.

The fabric of the chair is green with a raised design of ropey twirls that I trace with my finger while staring at the broken window. Not *broken* broken, like the air isn't blowing through. It's just a small set of cracks nestled in the bottom left corner like a dead spider. I stare at it and trace, stare and trace, and the voices of my family in the waiting room become the hum of a busy hive. A lulling drone. I know what they're saying; I've heard it all again and again and again.

"It's cancer," says my sister, as she clickity-clicks on her laptop some more.

"Liver and stomach."

I look up from the spot on the carpet that has been hypnotizing me and scan her face. I stick my reddened finger into my mouth. My eyes threaten to leak, so I bite down on my finger and look back to the floor.

"It's bad," she whispers.

She is a strong one, big kahuna of nurses at a hospital in Hawaii. She has impeccable bedside manner. However, every bedside is not of the bed containing your father. Her eyes are wet and her cheeks taut, aching from swallowing sobs. I know this look because I'm doing the same but not nearly as successful. My lips shake and I mumble a soft "Oh."

She holds out a hand and I take it and we quietly cry. Not as quietly as we think. We stopped trying to be strong on the third time through this.

My brother stands over in the corner, quiet and frowning. He has done his best to try and remove himself from it all. He has failed miserably. Our other sister sits with her young daughter and plays upbeat. We're waiting for our older sister to arrive from Maryland. My stepmother is back in the room with Dad. We go in shifts; I sit and cry and secretly hope my shift is a long way off. I wish I were hungry.

I go back to the carpet spot and think. Well, try to think, I start with a vision of Dad, back when I was little, but within seconds it has mutated into a sprawling white expanse filled with the sound of tears and snatches of dialogue from a lifetime of conversations with my father. His wonderfully raspy laugh. His deep timbered "Oh yeah?" when I would tell him something new. The "Love you" that ended every phone call or when coupled with a strong hug, every visit. I could see him, sitting at his kitchen table, cigarette smoking in the ashtray as he read the paper or one of his Civil War books. I can remember when he didn't look so old. Dark hair and dark mustache, so intense and serious. A contrast to how he was in personality. He stayed that way until the end, although the dark had given way to gray years before.

He knew what was coming. I am certain he did. He so desperately wanted to not burden anyone, he kept the discomforts and fears bottled until there was no other choice. My youngest sister found him, couch-bound and ill the day after Thanksgiving, and got him to the ER...and it all went to shit from there. We spent days there, waiting for our chance to visit. At first, it was the liver or stomach and they'd be able to possibly remove it and treat it. Then, after the first surgery, the grim reality was announced: the cancer was everywhere. They said they would try chemo as soon as he was strong enough. And eventually, they sent him home. Through it all, he never complained. Other than to wish he had a pizza, a personal-sized buffalo chicken pizza.

They finally sent him home, on my birthday.

In less than a week, he was back in the hospital. He had managed to get his pizza but hadn't been able to keep it down. Within a few days of being readmitted to the hospital, it was decided there wasn't much to be done. He was unconscious more than awake. My stepmother spent every night on the floor by his side. He was sent home to spend his final days with us. It was Christmas weekend.

I know it is something every person goes through, losing a parent. And as horrific and painful as it was, I would never trade the experience for anything. Holding my father's slender hand and tracing the tattoo that lived there with my shaking thumb. Watching his ragged breathing as he slept and internally pleading with him to know how very much I loved him. Leaving to allow someone else to come in and do the same. And then finally, being able to hold onto him, all of us, his wife and children, and let him know we would be okay, that he was free to go...and then watching the final heaving breath as he did just that. It was heartbreaking and magical and tragically beautiful at the same time. Something so simultaneously painful and special.

Until reality set in.

There was such a void left behind. We didn't know what to do. I sat back, and as the funeral director's men zipped him up and carried him out, I pushed my thumbs into my eyes until the spots danced. I listened to the blinding white, the voices and the sound of crying. I begged for them to stop.

I open my eyes and I am sitting in the green chair. Tracing the pattern. My stepmother comes out of the room, face wet and shiny.

"Johnny, you can go back if you want. You too, Roscoe."

I look to my brother, who just nods and as I snake my arm across his broad back, we walk down the hall.

"This sucks," he says.

"It most certainly does," I agree. Attempting a laugh that sputters and dies on my lips, we walk through the doors. Again.

I'm not sure which one of us made it this way. I cannot say whose grief was so strong that this was the answer to a prayer. We all wanted more time with Dad, but to have to go through this last month over and over...I don't know. I hope it wasn't me. I hope I didn't harbor such a wish in my heart. Secrets and dragons live there. I guess, some secrets *are* dragons. I pray this wasn't one of mine.

"Hello," Dad says weakly as we enter.

He looks like he's made of gray paper. He's gaunt and there's a pleading in his eyes. My mind sobs, *"My God, he knows. What are we doing to him?"*

But then he grabs my hand and squeezes it. "I love you boys. I've always been so proud of you..." and he manages a weak but warm smile. The eighty-second one I've seen since I started keeping track.

I squeeze it back and smile, tasting tears as they roll over my trembling lips. I've swallowed an ocean by now.

I cry, like it was the first time. Always like it was the first time. I almost wish it was.

THE TRICK

EVERY HALLOWEEN either Roscoe or I went as a hobo/old man/ bum. It was the easiest costume for Mom to whip up as it wasn't too far removed from our daily uniform. Worn jeans/pants, ratty shoes, and a big old flannel shirt. Usually stuffed with a pillow. We were always warned to keep the pillow clean and undamaged as it would be returned to the case and its place on our bed when we got home. We'd then take our brown paper bag and walk the length of our block. The faces of our neighbors usually a cocktail of thinly veiled disdain or snotty or sad embarrassment. It took me years to realize there was an ironic joke here.

Roscoe and I were always brothers, but we weren't always friends. We loved one another, but I couldn't say we were nice to one another. There was five years between us and a lot of circumstances;

often it felt like lifetimes and fathoms deep. Our father left when I was almost seven and Roscoe was two. There was a rocky valley forged in the fact I had a father for a few years, years I could and can recall somewhat fondly, while Roscoe had only a few splintered recollections of a man holding him as a baby. Once Dad left, we moved around for three years, like gypsies, the not-so-politically-correct term was—and during it all I found myself more primed for the role of surrogate parent/caregiver to this bullheaded little boy who squinted when he smiled and followed me like a shadow. It was a role I'd never auditioned for and had most definitely sought to lose. A role I realize now had bounties unforetold and riches unparalleled.

That joke being that we grew up in a poor area in the mountains of Pennsylvania. No one was rich or swimming in wealth. There were the dirt poor, the poor and those who were not as poor as the rest. I always felt we were the level above dirt. Most folks were good people. Hardworking parents. Most kids just happy to play and have fun. But some were cut from different, more expensive cloth. I vividly recall a girl telling me in third grade (after making fun of my Dollar Store vinyl hi-tops) that "If you don't wear Lee jeans or Nike sneakers, you're nothing." That is a false statement, but it sure made little Johnny feel like a little pile of nothing. I never told anyone about that. My mom already had her hands full—multiple jobs, keeping a house around us and food on the table all while holding up the world. There always had to be someone who looked down on those with less. And I'm not talking about money specifically.

As time crawled on, I found myself bitter at my lot in life. I wanted nothing more than to be a normal kid, to play with the others my age and to experience the pains and aches of growing up. I was in no way spared the aches, but probably had some the other kids didn't; I always had to factor in when Mom left for work so I could be home to watch my brother. How to cook and clean the house. To do laundry, check homework, and many other tasks that my friends' mothers or fathers handled for them. Mothers that didn't work, or if they did, only one job. Our mom was a nurse at night and cleaned houses during daylight hours, and on off nights from those, tended bar at the American Legion. For her hard work she was labeled a slut and a bad mother. Neither title being true, but basically being tongue-carved into the trunk of our lives. I grew older and meaner to Roscoe. Endless name calling and fighting. And while he fought back, he was always quick to forgive and return to his usually accepting love of his big brother.

This year I was going to go as a mummy. Mom had sacrificed one of our white sheets, as had Gram, to be torn into long strips of ancient bandage. It was the best costume I'd ever had. This year would be so much better.

Better than the cardboard box robot that got me condescending snickers from other children, some hard candy, tootsie rolls, and a stale popcorn ball.

Better than the cheap plastic masks with the rubber band that held them on your head but pulled at the hair at the back of your neck.

Better than seeing the looks on the faces of children who were nice to you once in a while, when there was no one else around. Children whose parents were still together and both worked and brought in more income than our poor three job holding mother did. Yeah, it would be better.

Years swirled and got away. I got married and moved across the state, won the role of a happy husband with two sons—a role I still play. Roscoe was married and had a pair of daughters. He tried to cut the leash to our hometown but never could. He was a boomerang. I always did what I could to help him when called to, or even when not. We rarely talked, but when we saw each other, it seemed strained a little. The elastic had dried and cracked like an old rubber band. I assumed it a resentment for the hand life dealt us, differing and wide in expanse. Too many small wounds from things I'd said or done when we were younger, given to salty scars that throbbed when I came around. When our grandmother died and then a few years later our father, those somber events strengthened our bond in some way. We still have our moments of antagonism but mostly we just quietly accept each other. We are brothers and that cannot be changed. We vowed to call more often and see each other more. We both treat vows like a juggler treats delicate glass.

The air was chilly, not cold but chilly. Mom said I'd need to wear my long johns under my costume, but not to get them dirty or torn as they were my only pair of pajamas until she could afford us new ones. I stood in the kitchen while Mom knelt in front of me, carefully wrapping my legs in linen. Gram sat at the table and smoked her cigarette. When the wrapping was done, I was covered head to toe, save for an opening left over my eyes so I could see. I ran into the living room and took in my costume via the full-length mirror. It was fabulous.

Gram said she'd drive us around. "Johnny will break his neck over them bandages around his ankles."

We got our bags and headed out.

First stop was old Mr. Whiteall. He sat on his porch swing with a large mixing bowl full of butterscotch discs and cinnamon lozenges. He always smelled sweaty but was a nice man.

"The Mummy walks!" he yelled, and shrank away in mock terror.

I laughed and took the offered treats. As we turned to leave his porch, a few boys from school passed in the opposite direction. One of them hissed, "Welfare Johnny."

I pretended not to hear.

The night was an apple halved—a sweetly tart and raw wound sticky at the same time. Gram sat in the car and smoked while Roscoe and I hit the houses, most adults smiling and handing us candy and compliments. Once in a while, some just looked at us like we'd shit on their porch and dropped the treats in our bags like used Kleenex. We went home and Gram left us to organize our spoils while Mom got ready for work.

Now, these decades later, I sit in my chair with the lights out, as I do every Halloween, and stare at the phone. It's right *there*. Inches from my hand. It'd be such an easy thing to pick it up and call my brother. Sometimes you'd think the device was made of spiders and bees—a cursed idol carved of scorpion sting and snakebite the way we eschew it. I sigh and don't make a move, choosing instead to once again take a walk through the territory behind my eyes.

"You made quite a haul!" Mom crowed as she grabbed a peanut butter chew from Roscoe's pile. I offered her one of my starlight mints.

"No, those are your favorite. You keep them." She went into the kitchen and got her sweater from the back of the chair. Crushed her cigarette to death in the ashtray on the table.

"Don't you kids eat all that candy tonight." She finished her coffee in a single gulp and sat the mug in the sink. It clattered with dirty silverware. "One more piece each, then brush and go to bed." We nodded. She reminded me for the millionth time to lock the door behind her when she left. I stood and watched her pull out into the road and the taillights disappeared into the night. We ate more than one piece of candy each and we went to bed without brushing our teeth. And the world never stuttered in its turning.

I often think of my brother and the years wasted between us. How all I need to do is call him once in a while, or even message him on the computer. In this day and age is there any valid excuse? I got pictures of the girls in the mail last week. They've grown up so much and I've not seen a lot of it. I'm as much a shadow to them as I am to him. A pre-diagnosed stranger. I look at the table where the pictures lay and can see the face of my brother in them. I see his school pictures in my mind. Green sweater and those squinting eyes when he smiled. He looks so happy. I so wish I could see him smile like that again. A smile that doesn't know what a spiteful prick the world is. What a vicious bitch life can be. And how the sharpest blade is the slow scalpel of time and apathy. I feel my eyes begin to leak and wipe them across my arm. The tears are cold on my warm skin. I smile and stare at the spot of light near the front window, a feeble sliver from the streetlight. I can almost see a short shadow by the chair. See the alfalfa sprout of Roscoe's perpetual cowlick. I see his eyes twinkle in the dim.

"What're you thinking about, Johnny?"

"Bandages."

"Like your mummy costume?"

"Not exactly."

"Like when you're hurt?"

"Often."

"Like what?"

"Like everything."

His small hand closes on mine.

"I love you."

"I love you too, little brother."

The streetlight goes dark and it thunders silence. I sit in it with my hand on the phone.

THE ONE WHO
HOLDS THE DOOR

MANY ARE those who spend their childhood longing for the day when they can free themselves of the bonds of their station. That station being the hometown they've been shackled to and hate even though deep down that's not likely to be true. They stare at the horizon and pine for the day they can be shot from it, like an arrow flying high and far and landing at some other spot on the grand map. Any other spot. There are also some who end up like boomerangs, trying as hard as they can to follow the lofty arrow's arc but are instead destined to swing and swoosh back to where they began. Oh, it's often not as immediate as that, or even as blatant. But it happens. I know because my baby brother Roscoe is a boomerang.

After several attempts at trying different directions—art school, full-time labor, and even a brief stumble through Bible college—he had gotten a job as a nurse's aide at the local VA while living in Pittsburgh. I heard numerous tales of tragedy and woe secondhand from his lips. The patients—is that what they call them? I don't know...people have always found Roscoe *easy*. His soul is neon kind...it blinks and calls to you to lay your burdens and fret down and just talk to him. A balm to the weary and weathered. The big boy with the big smile is now a large man with doe brown eyes, always slightly sad even when sitting above a smile. A smile that usually wishes for a cigarette or to open and let the screaming out.

"Was an old vet there. We called him Moses. He was wrinkled and black. His face resembled a raisin with a smile. He was the sweetest, even when he talked about the horrible things he'd seen and the more horrible things he'd done. He'd hold your fingers in his leathery hand and squeeze gently when needed. He'd tear up as he spoke and lick his lips often, and he always thanked me before I left. I made sure to thank him back, even if his tales made me believe he felt he didn't deserve it."

Roscoe made his way back to our small town over a decade ago, closing in on two, with a wife and daughter in tow, and another daughter not yet written into the script.

On the outer lip of town sits the Willow Home, an elder care facility to the refined; an old folks' home to the rest of us.

Roscoe took a job there, once more donning his nurse's aide cape, and it is there he has been working ever since. What started as a means to earn a paycheck and a job that afforded him his *deep-seated-even-if-he-never-admitted-it-to-himself* need to assist people is now a millstone of sorts—one he willingly yokes himself to every shift.

See, old folks' homes are vile necessities. In the modern world, it's not a feasible idea to assume everyone has the ability to take care of their own when age whittles them down, or illness takes a biting swing. And even if the mental wherewithal exists, sometimes it lacks the sturdy backing or the finances to see it through. And then one must consider the logistics. And yes, certainly there are some people who just want to be shut of the burden and foist it off on the men and women in the care business. Scribble the checks for a clean schedule and a spoonful of guilt once in a while. Maybe.

"Johnny, It's getting harder and harder to deal with the gig, man." Roscoe *sighs, and I can visualize the smoke frothing from his nostrils even over the phone.*

What Roscoe hadn't considered then, but a fact that seemed to smack him daily now, was that he was taking a job in an old folks' home. Well, yes, he had considered that part, but it was the fact this was his hometown—that was the part that sneered at him now. In the beginning, it was the usual level of tough. Taking care of those in the dusk of their lives, making them happy and comfortable for as long as possible before the end came. And that part has never gotten less arduous.

But now, Roscoe takes care of his history and his past. It's a somber *This Is Your Life* game he can't win or stop playing. The beds are now filled with old teachers or the parents and grandparents of friends. Every sick and aged face belongs to someone he's known practically his whole life, and even if they were not all pleasant fixtures, they were fixtures indeed.

"Old Tony Gellini is in the Willow now. That guy was always such a fucking dick. He hated us for no reason other than we were poor...or that you had long hair and liked loud music and scary movies...'Member, he's the one who started telling people you were a devil worshipper? Yeah, he's lost both legs to diabetes and has to be hooked up to oxygen. He can't go anywhere. And I have to take care of his sorry ass every shift. The misery he caused for no reason other than being a petty soul, and I go in there and smile and gently turn him and change his bedding or his bandages. I bring his food and tuck him in. And I smile. Sometimes I'm afraid my face is gonna break."

I don't talk to Roscoe as much as I'd like and I see him even less. When we do talk, we talk fast and furious.

"I get to take care of Ray's grandma. She's in her 90s and is the

sweetest thing. Sometimes she swears and then giggles and covers her mouth like a schoolgirl and tells me to make sure I don't tell Ray."

"Old Mr. Janis was in last winter, remember him, he was our old Biology teacher? He'd had a stroke and then his kidneys faded and he just went down from there. But I took care of him, and we talked a good bit. He remembered you. Asked about you. Asked me if you still wrote your stories. Told me about how he had to paddle you in eighth grade. He was so small at the end..." Roscoe paused and crushed out the cigarette between his fingers. *"We all are."*

And then we hug...and that's my favorite part. When my little brother encircles me in his big arms and squeezes. I feel so safe in it. I feel like maybe you really can go home again.

I got to see my brother a few weeks ago. And I asked him how work was going. After telling me about mandatory overtime and budget cuts and governmental bullshit which put images of elephants balancing on pool cues in my head, he told me this story:

"Missus Winston passed away the other week. She taught fourth grade over at the elementary school. We both had her. She was in her eighties, a little younger than Gram. She was a little thing, (he chuckles here) I held her in one arm when I made her bed. Anyway, I was bed checking and as I went to leave, she spoke, calling me back to her bedside."

"Rossy," she called. "Some doors was made to slam and others to close gently. Some doors ain't even doors at all, just terrible windows."

"What does that even mean?" he said.

She smiled, her teeth shining like new chalk. "It means when time is eatin' yer dust, son, and the only movin' forward you're doing is slow and slower. You need someone to steady you. To know the door you want, the one you need, and guide you to it and hold it for you." Her eyes softened and she laid a twiggy hand on my forearm, just below the tattoo there. I think I even smiled myself, a little.

"You can hold the door for me then," she whispered as she loosened her grip.

I barely noticed. I looked down at her face, a sketch in wrinkle and scribbled line, and I smiled deep and genuine.

"It's what I'm here for," I said, and patted her arm, just under the bruise from her IV. Her eyes closed and soft snores fluttered about the room. I walked to the door and flicked the lights to dim, turning to get one more look at the sleeping Mrs. Winston.

"It's my privilege," I whispered to her. "And my curse."

The silence that swarmed the room after he spoke was monstrous. I looked at him as he stared out the window with wet eyes and a straight-line smile. He absently picked up his coffee cup and sipped, swallowing loudly. He turned and looked at me, a real smile now beaming.

"How you doing, Johnny?"

AUTHOR NOTES

I SHALL assume that if you are reading these that you have, in fact, finished the book and aren't skipping ahead. That's what we consider cheating and there will no doubt be a few spoilers here, so this is your final warning.

Jedi Summer With The Magnetic Kid began its life as a flash fiction story called "The Magnetic Kid" and it was basically the chapter where Roscoe walks down the street trailed by the train of ghost pets. The more I meddled with it, the more I decided I wanted to do something more with it, with us and our childhood. I knew that a lot of folks would be able to relate to varying aspects of the story. I also knew from the onset that it would not be a traditional arc or narrative. There would be no real answers and the end would just simply be a moment...that's how life is sometimes.

Almost everything in this story happened, exceptions being the Ferris wheel incident and *some* of the ghostly business. There was never a corpse in the trees, lest one we discovered. Pretty much all the other oddness is factual. I swear.

I wrote it in a specific candor; there are repeated uses of that's and that and same words in sentences. That's how kids talk and think, and even though this story is told by adult me, the mindset or view on the past by drifting back there, oh to hell with it...I wrote it the way it felt right to.

"Possessed By A Broken Window" also began as a short story, subbed to and accepted for Apokrupha Press's Lamplight magazine. I believe issue 3, volume 3. That story wrung me the hell out. It is 100% accurate save for the time loop...is there a time loop or does grief just keep dragging you around in a way that it feels like it? There were tears shed during the writing, and the summer I chose this as my piece to read at the Scares That Care convention, it wrecked the room. Grief and tears are the best equalizer, I suspect.

"The Trick" was written at the ask of Gabino Iglesias. He was looking for content for a blog series of Halloween pieces and I wrote and subbed this to him. It was never used, so I sent it out the next fall to Meghan Hyden for her to run on her blog. I came up with the idea when I was sitting in the dark, thinking about my brother and how easy it would be to call him and yet, I never do. Memories are a stream that always runs, sometimes deep and fast, and other times brackish and shallow.

"The One Who Hold The Door." This piece was written fresh for the ill-fated Poltergeist edition of *Jedi*. It wound up in the Thunderstorm/Nightworms limited and now, it lives here. When asked if I could write a new "Johnny & Roscoe" bit...I drew a blank as I often do. Then I started thinking about a recent visit with my brother, who is a nurse in the old folks' home on the edge of our hometown. The piece just came out, and I wish there was more fiction to it than there is.

ABOUT THE AUTHOR

My brother Ross and I,
Christmas 1982

JOHN BODEN lives a stone's throw from Three Mile Island with his wonderful wife and sons. A baker by day, he spends his off time writing, watching TV, or laughing with his wife. He likes Diet Pepsi, cheeseburgers, heavy metal, and sports ferocious sideburns. While his output as a writer is fairly sporadic, it has a bit of a reputation for being unique. He owes an unpayable debt to Ken Wood who invited him along at the start of Shock Totem and that singular act rckindled his love for writing, after ignoring it for 20 years. His books include: Dominoes, Spungunion, Walk The Darkness Down as well as the collaborative novellas Out Behind The Barn (with Chad Lutzke), Rattlesnake Kisses, Cattywampus and the forthcoming Black Salve (with Robert Ford) and Detritus In Love (with Mercedes M. Yardley). He thanks you from the bottom of his hairy heart, sincerely.